PIES, POTIONS AND PERIL

LILA HARROW: A POINT MUSE COZY PARANORMAL MYSTERY BOOK TWO

KELLY ETHAN

 Created with Vellum

Pies, potions, and a bake sale battle to the death. Let the mayhem begin.

Lila Harrow, baker witch extraordinaire, had one hard and fast rule. Stay away from bake sales.

Because baking can be murder.

Now thanks to her hex-loving, blackmail-wielding grandmother, Elspeth Harrow, Lila's stuck as a judge for the annual Point Muse Academy's Founding Day bake sale.

But when the competition heats up and the body

count rises, what's Lila to do but add a little spice to the mix and solve a murder.

A piece of cake for a witchy baker.

If you like snarky dialogue, murder and mayhem then you'll love the second installment in Kelly Ethan's Point Muse Cozy Paranormal Mystery spin off series – Lila Harrow: A Point Muse Cozy Paranormal Mystery!

<u>Unlock the mayhem of Pies, Potions and Peril.</u>

ONE

"This is torture. Has to be against the Geneva Convention." Lila Harrow, baker-witch extraordinaire, closed one eye and winced as the teenage wannabe hit a shrill note.

"I'm pretty sure the Geneva Convention doesn't cover school talent shows." Holly Harrow, half Banshee-half witch, nudged her cousin. "Now, hush. I like this song."

"What song? All I can hear is a series of notes threaded together with a teenage high-pitched whine." Xandie Meyers, Librarian to the supernatural Great Library of Alexandria, and another of Lila's cousins, joined in critiquing the teenager's performance.

"Right on, cuz." Lila fist-pumped her cousin.

Xandie and Holly had joined her in solidarity and shared misery, except for her vocally confused cousin, Holly, who enjoyed the show. All three Harrow cousins shared the witchy Harrow genes, including an insatiable curiosity and the Harrow amber eyes, along with brown hair and a habit of finding the odd corpse...or two.

"Shush," Holly hushed her cousins, and sat forward, eyes trained on the stage.

"This is all Elspeth's fault." Her hex-loving, wicked witch grandmother, Elspeth Harrow, had blackmailed Lila into attending the week-long festivities of Point Muse Academy's Founding Day celebrations. Just because of a tiny incident of wig stealing, followed by a drunken tabletop can-can.

"You shouldn't have stolen one of Elspeth wigs. You know how obsessed she gets over them." Holly wiped her eyes. "That performance wowed me. Who knew Point Muse Academy could produce such an artist at the annual talent show?"

"Or how tone deaf you are." Lila glanced around the school hall. The Academy had been founded at the same time as the town, in the late seventeen hundred. Because the town sat on a nest of ley lines, supernatural creatures flocked to the area. Three descendants of the nine muses ran the Academy as head mistresses. Clio and Mel were cool, but Calliope had a snooty streak a mile wide. The town was a mix of cute wooden gables and ancient stone, and the Academy was no different. The hall featured a stage at one end, highly polished wooden floorboards, and a cupola above that acted as a skylight. The walls had a mix of engraved wooden panels with images of muses frolicking. The town's over-privileged teens attended side-by-side with the rest of the town's offspring, but money definitely wasn't short at the Academy.

Speaking of the town teenagers... Lila spied Es Penne, teenage dragon and sometimes bakery assistant, creeping toward the stage. Nudging Xandie, Lila whispered, "Chaos is afoot." She pointed to the skulking teenager.

"I don't think her grandmother would approve."

Lila snorted. "Marjorie is a poker crony of Elspeth's. She probably encouraged the mayhem."

Es crept along the side of the hall, away from spectators. She raised a hand, aimed at the purple glitter-covered petite blonde on the stage and let loose.

Lila watched as a small transparent balloon landed at the singer's feet. Immediately, smoke gushed out and covered her legs, then quickly wreathed the singer's form before spreading over the stage.

The dragon teenager plastered herself against the wall as smoke covered her as well.

"That's my queue for a refreshment break." Lila stood and threaded her way along the aisle toward Es. Without waiting for her cousins, she surged forward. Lila Harrow to the rescue. In the past Lila and Holly had indulged in way too many pranks at the Academy not to want to rescue a fellow rule breaker.

A willowy woman with blue flowing locks clambered onto the stage and spoke into the microphone. "If everyone could please exit the room carefully, we'll break for refreshments." She placed a hand over the microphone and had a fierce whispered conversation with another woman with brightly colored hair.

Lila reached the wall where she'd last seen Es and extended a hand into the thickest part of the cloud. She latched onto an arm and yanked.

Es muffled a shriek as she fell against Lila when the baker pretended to hug her.

"Walk with me casually, like you never emptied the room with an Elspeth-made smoke bomb."

Promenading with linked arms, Lila winked at

her cousins as they joined the hide-Es-Penne conga line.

"You can't pin anything on me." Es faked a smile as she passed glaring teachers.

"Except the fact I watched you do it and recognized Elspeth's creative handiwork."

"No way," Es hissed. "She gave me an invisibility paste. No possible way you could have seen me."

As they headed into a foyer where refreshments were set up, Lila leaned closer and squeezed the girl's arm. "Lesson number one. Elspeth Harrow lies, it creates more mayhem, and therefore is even more entertaining."

"Aw, man," Es groused and kicked a black boot-shod foot out like a petulant child.

The dragon stood at just over five feet and had long straight black hair with one single white strip. Dressed all in black, the only proper color was her brightly painted neon nails and ice blue eyes. Lila released the teenager's arm as Xandie and Holly gathered around.

"When in doubt, deny, deny, deny. That's the Harrow motto," Xandie said.

"I thought that was never get caught?" Holly frowned.

"That too." Lila considered the pouty girl in

front of her. "Why wait until that purple girl opened her mouth to smoke bomb her?"

Es curled her lip. "Marion Sylvis. Bunny shifter and mean girl of the school. She deserved it."

"Esmeralda Penne! Anything to confess?" A blue-tressed, willowy woman crossed her arms and glared at the dragon.

Es flicked her long black hair over her shoulder. "Clean conscience, Ms. Calliope. You?"

The woman swelled in stature and took a deep breath, but before she could say anything, Lila shoved Xandie forward. "Calliope, have you met Xandie Meyers, my cousin, yet? She's the Librarian to the Great Library of Alexandria. Don't you have a personal family connection to the Library?"

Calliope, a descendant of one of the nine muses who'd helped establish the original Library in ancient Alexandria, opened and closed her mouth before she pasted a smile on her face. "Ms. Meyers, it's an honor to meet you. The Muses have always had a close relationship with the Library." She paused and arched an eyebrow. "You did know the Library was founded as a tribute to my family? We have a vested interest in its presence here in Point Muse." The teenager all but forgotten, the muse shouldered Lila out of the way. "I would love to give you a tour of our little oasis of educational paradise." She clutched Xandie's arm and led her off.

Xandie peeked around the muse's shoulder and mimed *help me* at Lila, who just waved. "And that is how a Harrow rescue and distraction mission is carried out." Lila dusted her hands off.

"And you tossed your own cousin under the Muse bus to do it. Elspeth would be proud of you," Holly sneered.

Es bowed her head. "I acknowledge your superior gifts of subterfuge and mayhem. I will endeavor to learn at the altar of Harrow greatness." She ruined the effect by snorting laughter.

"Brat." Lila flicked the mouthy kid's nose. "Why don't you blend into the crowd and avoid that mean bunny shifter. If she works out what you did, she'll hunt you down and then nibble your ankles to death."

"You have no clue how vicious bunny shifters really are. Marion goes for the throat before she'd lower herself to attack the ankles." Es rolled her eyes but followed Lila's advice and blended into the crowd as much as a goth teenage dragon could.

"Are we positive her last name isn't Harrow?"

"Pretty sure there's no dragons in the Harrow ancestry. Wicked witches, yes. Dragons, no." Lila dragged Holly toward the refreshments. "Let's check out the food. Es told me the catering class made everything. I want to see how good they are." Lila grabbed a shrimp puff and chewed with a thoughtful expression. "Light, tasty. I give this an A plus."

Holly grabbed a grilled chicken skewer and nibbled. "Pretty good."

Lila perused the food table. "Mini brioche lobster rolls, blueberry salsa, crab cakes, red pepper bruschetta and chicken skewers. Interesting choice for a school talent show."

"This is the premier supernatural Academy in North America, Ms. Harrow."

Lila gulped and swiveled to face a fate worse than Elspeth. *Emmaline Winchester!* She almost groaned out loud. "Ah, Ms. Winchester. Nice to see you." A no-nonsense, steel-spined, greying redhead glared at Lila with piercing emerald green eyes. "Not nice to be here when such mayhem is occurring, but these are teenagers. Probably local riffraff from the town."

A short woman, with black-rimmed glasses and bright red, wildly curling hair, shoved out a hand and shook Lila's. "Hi. I'm Edie Winchester. Emmaline's Great-Niece."

Lila smiled at the eager woman. "Lila Harrow. This is my cousin, Holly."

"I figured. You look alike. I'm an only child, no siblings or close cousins, unfortunately."

"It ain't all it's cracked up to be." All three Harrow cousins shared the same brown hair and amber Harrow eyes, but thankfully that's where it ended. Lila, the eldest, had long curly brown hair, way too many curves and a tendency toward dramatics. Hence the nickname of *drama llama Lila*. Xandie, the middle cousin, with average height, had shoulder length frizzy brown hair, a bookish inclination and was stubborn to a fault. Holly, the youngest and shortest of cousins, had no curves to speak of, a chin length brown bob and was quieter and more death-obsessed, perfectly natural for a half banshee who worked in a funeral home.

"I guess you know my Great-Aunt." Edie gestured over a shoulder at a dumpy dour-faced middle-aged woman who stood behind Emmaline Winchester's wheelchair. "This is Mildred. She looks after my Great-Aunt."

"Edith," the elderly Winchester remonstrated. "One doesn't introduce the staff in public, or private for that matter. We do have a standing in Point Muse, something even a Harrow should understand." Emmaline sniffed then completely ignored the Harrows and clicked her fingers at the woman behind her.

The snooty Winchester matriarch wheeled past with the sour-faced Mildred walking briskly. A strong smell of lavender-scented perfume wafted around Lila and threatened to choke the life out of her senses. She cleared her throat and grabbed another shrimp puff. "Another quality interaction with the grand-dame of the social putdown."

"Lila," Holly choked out her cousin's name.

Lila spotted Edie still standing next to them. "Whoops, sometimes my mouth and my brain short-circuit."

She smiled lopsidedly. "It's okay. I haven't had much to do with my Great-Aunt until a week ago. I've been looking at the family tree and decided to visit since she only lived a few hours away from my parents."

Holly winced. "And you're still here?" Holly bit her lip. "Sorry, that sounded like Lila way too much."

"Hey." Lila dug her cousin in the ribs. "No need for sassy. Emmaline has a reputation in Point Muse and doesn't suffer fools gladly."

"I'm finding that out. My side of the family hasn't had anything to do with the Point Muse

Winchesters in years and years. I'm starting to realize why. But I guess if you're a green witch, trapped in a wheelchair and can't get outside to garden, I'd be grumpy too."

"You're a witch like Emmaline?" Lila probed the newcomer. She seemed nice enough, but with Winchester genes, who knew?

Edie nodded with a smile. "I'm not the greatest greenie out there, but I do love growing things. I'm a bit of an aberration within the Winchesters as I also collect snakes. Emmaline won't let me keep them in Winchester House, but the school's kindly letting me board them here. Besides, the students love studying them."

Holly shivered. "You're brave. They scare me. Give me the walking dead any day."

"That happens here a lot? The walking dead, I mean."

"You'd be surprised." Lila shrugged. "Holly's part Banshee, part Witch, and works at the Elysian Fields Funeral home. I have a bakery in town, and I'm obsessed with sugar, not dead people."

"Oh, *Heart's Delight*. I've been there. Your chocolate brownies are amazing."

Lila grimaced. "Let's not talk about brownies, it traumatizes me."

"Edith. Attend, please."

The trio of women hunched their shoulders as Emmaline's strident tones filled the air.

"Nice meeting you. I'll see you when I need my next sugar hit." She shot the Harrows a genuine smile as she rushed off to her great-aunt.

"Poor thing, dancing attendance on that battleax."

"Lila Marie Harrow, be nice. If she hears you, you're in for it." Holly slapped Lila on the back. "I'm going to wander. Meet you inside for round two of the talent show when it lets back in."

"Not if I'm lucky it won't." Lila waved her cousin off and wandered around the room, nodding to acquaintances. She found an empty hallway near an alcove and breathed a sigh of relief. Elspeth, her grandmother and head of the Harrow family of witches, may have bribed her to turn up and represent, but Lila never agreed to enjoy it.

"I know exactly what you've done. What would the residents of Point Muse say if they knew how low you would stoop?"

A woman's high-pitched whine caught Lila's attention. She pretended to read the talent show program attached to the wall next to her. Someone replied in a muffled tone. Lila strained to hear the words.

"You do care. The town would shun you. If you don't want that to happen, you better do exactly what I want, or Founding Day celebrations will be far more exciting than they normally are."

The high-pitched voice trailed off as if the woman speaking had moved away. Lila counted to twenty before she eased away from the wall and poked her head around the alcove. The hallway was completely empty of any stray blackmailers or victims. Because that's exactly what that conversation had sounded like. "Blackmail. Another jewel in the crown of Point Muse tourism."

They just needed a body now...

TWO

"Do you have to spread out so much? It looks like a tornado swept through here," Lila grouched and reorganized the papers on her desk.

"Called work, Harrow. Maybe you should try." Matthew Grim, Point Muse's very own reaper, winked at the grouchy baker. "What soured your milk?"

"Spending all day yesterday at the Academy's talent show." Lila waggled her finger at the attractive reaper's beaky nose. "That's ironic. *Talent show?* Because there wasn't any. The highlight of the day was Es Penne's smoke bomb and hearing someone get blackmailed in a deserted hallway. Otherwise, a truly wasted day."

Grim leaned against a desk shoved against the

wall of Lila's bakery office. "Should we be concerned?"

"Since *we* didn't hear it, *we* will be fine," Lila sniped back at the frowning reaper. Who'd have thought a frown would look so good on him. Matthew Grim was a large, solid man, with black hair, gray eyes and the aforementioned beaky nose. A tidy package that set the hearts of singles of both sexes aflame. But for some reason he stuck like a burr to Lila. He lived in the spare apartment above her bakery and his family had even set up a branch of the reaping business in Point Muse...in *her* office. And if she were honest, Lila might have felt a flutter or two herself when the reaper walked past.

"You're a Harrow. It's a quick step from black-mail to finding a body."

Lila slapped a hand on her desk. "I'm a baker. That's all. And bodies find Harrows. It's not like we create the drama."

"Just thrive off the energy."

"That's Elspeth." Lila sighed. "I swear I'm not actively looking for a crime. I just have to get through the next week and pay my Elspeth penance."

Grim smirked. "The can-can incident?"

"More like stealing her wig and having more fun than she did. My grandmother's petty like that."

Lila's dog, Nash, jumped up from his bed and Lila opened the door and let him into the bakery. Her Brownie assistant, Hester, would keep an eye on him. After growing up with her veterinarian empath mother, Amelia Harrow, and a house filled with animals, she vowed once she moved out that she'd never have a pet. That was until two prison-escaping demon sisters came hunting her and Hades gifted her with a hellhound puppy for protection. Now she couldn't imagine living without Nash. Except for maybe his love of icing and his habit of calling her his pet. She could live without either one of those issues.

"Just stay out of trouble. That's all I ask." The reaper made a show of tidying up his desk. "Happy now?"

"I'm ignoring you."

"Does that mean I don't get any *Vanilla Viagra for the Soul* cupcakes?"

Lila snorted and stepped into the bakery. "You don't need any Viagra for your soul. Your energy's fine."

"Spoilsport."

Ignoring the mouthy reaper, Lila wove her way through her bakery, smiling and nodding to customers as she went. The wood floors shone, and her large stone fireplace gave the room a warm atmosphere. White-painted wooden tables and chairs were dotted around the room and a large sofa in front of the hearth added to the ambience of the bakery. Two large bay windows looked out onto the quaint cobbled Main Street. *Heart's Delight Bakery* was all Lila's. She'd inherited very few witchy gifts except the ability to infuse her baked goods with Harrow magic. Her bakery had a reputation far and wide for its magical baked goods. Lila prided herself on delivering clarity of heart, mind, and soul in every baked goody she served. Need that positive energy to ask for a raise? Try *Vanilla Viagra for the Soul*. Need to make a decision but can't commit? Try Lila's *Commitment Coconut Slice*. And it was all hers.

"Earth to Lila?" Xandie leaned against the counter and flicked a piece of cupcake at Lila. "Dreaming of your reaper again?"

Lila snorted. "As if." Not the wittiest of Harrow comebacks, but she refused to admit to her meddling family just how interested she might be in Matthew Grim. "Is there a reason you're plaguing me, cousin?"

"The head mistresses of the Academy have invited me to attend a series of personal tours at the Academy. Since you're still paying out your Elspeth punishment, I thought we'd go together."

"So, you need a ride?"

"I need a ride."

"Give me five minutes. I have to let Hester know. She's training her niece to take over as the bakery assistant." Her last assistant, Janie, had been a victim of an obsessed killer. Lila pushed her regret to the side and poked her head into the kitchen. "Xandie and I are heading out to punishment central. You all good to go?"

The little Brownie sneered, her muscular shoulders twitching. "I've been ready since you were in your diapers, girl."

"That doesn't surprise me." Lila smiled at Hester's tiny blue-headed niece. "You think you can cope, Bronwyn?"

"What she said." Bronwyn pointed to her aunt. "But without the diaper bit. Yuck." She shuddered in horror.

"Okay then. If you need me, I'm at the school." A commotion in the bakery drew Lila back into the seating area. The bakery was open, and her hellhound had managed to wedge himself between Emmaline Winchester's wheelchair and the door. Edie knelt next to the whining puppy as the elderly Winchester complained.

"It's a health code violation. Animals should not

be allowed in food preparation and serving areas. It isn't sanitary."

"Sorry, Ms. Winchester. Nash is my guard dog. Something must have concerned him." Lila stood behind Edie and rubbed Nash's ears. "It's okay, pup. Edie will help you."

Nash whimpered, but submitted to the younger Winchester's ministrations.

Emmaline thumped her wheelchair armrest. "In my day, it would never have been allowed."

"In your day, there were horses and carts." Lila murmured under her breath and felt Edie shake with laughter.

"What did you say, Ms. Harrow?" Emmaline glared at Lila.

"Nothing. Hades himself appointed Nash as guard dog, so as such, we have a waiver from the Health Department so he can be available for security. With that settled, please do come and have a morning tea on the bakery. Free of charge."

"There you go, Mister Nash." Edie stood and dusted off her hands.

Nash pushed past Lila and bolted for the kitchen. Poor puppy had the right idea. Lila would bolt if she could too. "Thanks, Edie. He looks like a big dog but is still a puppy. Doesn't realize where his paws and tail go yet."

"He's a cutie, it was just a little tangle with Great-Aunt Emmaline's wheelchair."

"Enough chitchat, Edith. You grab our order. I shall wait outside. Park me, please."

Edie positioned her great-aunt to the side of the entrance, facing the opposite side of Main Street. "I won't be long."

"You better not be. We can't be late for the tours. The Winchesters have a reputation to uphold within the Academy."

Edie bit her lip and entered the bakery, closing the door with a solid thunk behind her."

"She's meaner than Elspeth."

"You have no idea. Sourest woman I have ever met. I can understand why the family kept their distance." Edie took a deep breath and exhaled slowly. "Can we get a couple cappuccinos to go and any cupcakes that sweeten a sour disposition?"

Lila winked. "I have just the thing. *Sugar and Spice and Make Me Nice Slice*. You heading to the tours?"

"Yep. Emmaline won't miss a day of the founding celebrations. Winchesters have a social reputation to uphold within Point Muse." She mimicked her great-aunt's upper crust tones perfectly.

Lila handed her the cupcakes. "The drinks will be a few minutes. I see the prison warden isn't dancing attendance today?"

"Mildred? She has errands to run, thankfully." Edie lowered her voice. "Frankly, the woman gives me the creeps. She's always there watching, but she does dote on Emmaline. So, that's something."

Speaking of the nasty spinster, Lila peered out her bakery window. Emmaline seemed happy enough parked outside, staring up and down the street, watching people. Two figures across the road near Bertie Boxwood's alchemy shop caught both Lila and Emmaline's attention. It wasn't often you saw a statuesque, skinny blonde looming over and waggling a finger in the face of a short, baldheaded man.

"More dramas in Point Muse?" Xandie wandered out of the kitchen and handed two cappuccinos over to Lila, who shrugged.

"He probably chipped her new nail polish and she's cursing him. Another day in Point Muse." Lila passed the drinks across to Edie. "There you go. We'll probably see you at the Academy soon."

"See you later." With a nod of thanks, Edie hurried out to her great-aunt.

"Right." Lila grabbed Xandie and shoved her back through the kitchen and out into the alley. "Are you ready for the *Heart's Delight Bakery* van experience?"

"Probably not." Xandie grimaced, but bravely climbed into the neon-colored van.

"Well, buckle up, buttercup. The ride's about to get wild." The ride might be wild but hopefully the Academy would be plain sailing.

"Why do we have to be in the group with finger-waving Barbie?" Lila whispered to Xandie as they trundled along the hallway with the rest of the tour.

"Because we had no choice?" Xandie answered and then hushed her cousin. "Just in case Elspeth gives you a pop quiz about the tour, you need to listen."

Lila curled her lip. "The day I study is the day the underworld freezes over, and Elspeth swears off mayhem. Speaking of our wicked witch grandmother, she's been suspiciously quiet after black-mailing my presence at the Academy." Lila glanced around the science lab. Even being banned from the celebrations, Elspeth always found a way into where she wasn't wanted. *Where was she?*

A perky teenager in a cheerleader costume, with a tiny kitten nestled in her arms, accidentally bumped into Lila. "I am *so* sorry. It's a bit crowded in here. Too many people are interested in the Academy. Seems like it's the place to be." The pretty brunette trilled a laugh and wandered off to the back of the room.

"What's wrong?" Xandie questioned her cousin.

Lila couldn't put a finger on it, but something about that teenager rubbed her the wrong way.

"A grandmother souring my mix." Lila waved Xandie's confusion away. "Don't worry. But you're right. We need to focus in case Elspeth grills us. I still expect her to pop up at any minute."

"I don't need to worry about studying. Not when we have a brainiac bunny with us." A tall blonde smirked and pointed to a petite brunette glaring at them from the other side of the room.

"Brainiac bunny?" Lila stared at the same woman who'd been finger-wiggling outside the alchemy shop this morning.

"She's a bunny shifter." The woman tossed her long blond hair over her shoulder and leaned in conspiratorially. "Brainiac used to geek out in the science labs when we were at school. Made the rest of us look like average students. As if that were possible." The woman smirked and waved to the bunny shifter before moving to the front of the tour next to the lab bench.

"Mean girl or what?"

"It's the Academy, Xandie. That was tame." Mean girls spawned everywhere in the world, but the Academy always had an excess of them. Thankfully, most people, especially the students at the Academy, had been too scared of Elspeth to do anything soul destroying to the teenage Lila and Holly.

"Well, I think the rivalry's still strong." Xandie pointed to the bunny shifter, who now stood a few steps behind the blonde, glaring at her shoulder blades.

"Excuse me, everyone. If you can gather close. We have a fantastic science experiment to show you." The bespectacled male science teacher in a lab coat gestured for them to come closer. "Now, if I could just have a volunteer?"

"Britney would love to volunteer. She loves the spotlight, but just has no clue how to spell the word."

The bunny shifter lurched forward and pushed the girl at the bench.

"The Academy would love the participation of Ms. Cygnus, our P.T.A. president." The teacher twitched a nervous smile at the group.

Giving in gracefully, the blonde woman stepped up next to the science teacher, who handed her a set of goggles

"Now I look like Chloe when we were in school. Remember that photo of you and your goggles in the yearbook? So cute." She bared her teeth at the other woman before the science teacher cut in.

"This year, we're lucky enough to have a snake enclosure on school property, thanks to Edith Winchester." The teacher gestured to the back of the room.

Lila turned and spotted Edie and Emmaline at the back of the room. She gave a wave before focusing back on the science teacher's talk.

"As you can see from our display board, we have learned quite a bit about snake biology and venom. The students were interested in what a reptile egg felt like, so we conducted an experiment." The teacher gestured to the objects on the bench. "We took a normal egg, placed in a glass, and then added vinegar and food coloring to it."

Lila peered at the lurid green egg that sat in the bubbling vinegar. She shuddered. The poor egg looked like an Elspeth hex potion gone wrong.

"Vinegar has bubbled and foamed around the egg. If you observe the size difference to a normal egg, you can see the vinegar has passed through the shell and caused the egg to swell." The teacher stepped back and motioned his volunteer forward. "If Ms. Cygnus would carefully remove the egg and cut it open, you can see how the vinegar and food coloring has permeated the shell."

"Bet swan girl's cursing her bunny torturer right now," Lila whispered.

"What swan girl?"

"The volunteer's name is Cygnus. Mean's she's a swan shifter," Lila pointed out to her cousin. "Swan shifters are mean. They're about the only people nasty enough to take on a bunny shifter."

"Aren't bunnies cute? What's scary about them?"

"Trust me, they aren't the lovable vegetable-nibbling animal everyone thinks they are." Lila shuddered. "I've seen a colony of rabbit shifter's strip the meat off an intruder in seconds."

The teenage cheerleader that stood close by hushed them.

The teacher let the swan shifter step forward and carefully lift out the egg onto the bench. He pointed to the shell. "If you touch it, you can feel how tough and pliable the leathery shell is. This simulates the feel of a reptile egg. If you could carefully cut the egg open?" The teacher stepped away to grab the trash can.

"It feels like my handbag." The woman giggled, and then concentrated as she carefully cut it open. The egg oozed a green viscous liquid. The shifter bent over and prodded the egg. Without warning, the egg exploded, covering the shifter's face, bare hands, and her arms. Screeching, she leapt back, as her skin started to smoke. "Get it off. Get it off. It's burning." She stumbled back as her smoking skin began to bubble. Then she let out a bloodcurdling wail and dropped to the floor behind the bench.

The science teacher stood frozen, the trash can still extended. The whole room remained silent, except for the gurgling of the mean girl on the floor behind the bench.

Lila shot forward and rushed behind the bench, Xandie and the blond cheerleader following. She leaned down next to the red-as-a-lobster, blistered woman and took her pulse.

"Is she okay?" The teenager had her kitten on

her shoulder, both peering down at the exploding egg victim.

Standing, Lila shook her head. "Xandie, you need to call Braun. Ms. Cygnus is dead."

Forget the blackmail, it was body time again in Point Muse...

THREE

"Why do I always find a Harrow near a body?" Zach Braun, police chief and Xandie's main squeeze, glared at Lila.

"Hey, I was just the first one to react. Nothing to do with either one of us." Poor Zach, he wasn't too far off the track to be honest. A murder in Point Muse almost always meant a Harrow involved. Originally, he'd fought to keep Xandie out of his investigations, but as a Librarian to the Great Library of Alexandria and a catalyst for mayhem, she was always in the thick of the action. Lila considered the bear shifter. He looked tired. Bags protruded under his pale blue eyes and his sandy hair hung limp. Maybe the chaos of Point Muse had finally gotten to him? "Time for a pick-me-up? You're looking ragged. Maybe I should bake you some honey cakes?"

"I wouldn't say no to more honey cakes. It's shedding season and the twins won't stop whining. I think it's time to move out." He rubbed a hand over his forehead and sighed mournfully.

The twins were Zach's deputies and his younger brothers, Caleb, and Riley. "Tell them if they don't stop bellyaching, I'll cut their honey cake supply off." Lila winked at the shifter.

"My poor baby," Xandie cooed and rubbed her boyfriend's back.

Lila fake gagged. "Way to spoil a friendly moment."

"My thoughts exactly." Matthew Grim closed the door of the science lab behind him.

Since the only people allowed in the lab were currently law enforcement, crime scene brownies and Lila and Xandie, why would a nosy reaper stick his nose into a death caused by an allergic reaction? She thought he only dealt with suspicious supernatural deaths.

"Following me?" Lila enquired with a saucy tilt of the head. You caught more sticky beaks with sugar rather than salt as Elspeth would say.

"She's dead and I'm a reaper. Work it out, Harrow." Grim ignored Lila and headed for the body, Braun close behind.

Both men crouched next to the dead shifter and murmured to each other.

"Point to him. He shut you down." Xandie licked a finger and pretended to draw a point in the air.

"Not a competition. I just assumed since it was an allergic reaction, he wouldn't be called in. It's Grand Central Station here. Next thing you know, death girl will turn up."

As if on cue, the door opened, and Holly strode in.

"See what I mean?" Lila threw her hands up and stomped closer to the bench.

"Hey, don't sass me. I'm here in an official capacity. Once the crime scene brownies are done, I have to cart the body off to the funeral home for the autopsy."

Lila shivered at the thought of Holly's twin necromantic bosses. They took freaky to a whole new level.

A silver glow peeped over the top of the bench before winking out after a few seconds. Matthew stood, his reaper scythe full-length in his hand.

"At least this time her soul's intact. I'll ferry this off. Keep an eye on the office." He winked at Lila. "I'll pop into the bakery and take Nash with me. He could do with some fresh air." The reaper headed out without waiting for Lila to respond.

Lila pushed the irritating way the reaper claimed her hellhound out of her mind and focused on Braun. "What next?"

He stood and waved in the crime scene brownies. "Holly waits until my brownies finish and then takes the body to autopsy. I interview everyone who was in the room and you get to hang around without getting into trouble." He shooed Xandie and Lila from the room. "Keep an eye and ear out. See if you can learn anything." He shut the door with Holly making funny faces behind his back.

Lila stepped forward. "I don't see why Holly has to stay."

"Calm, baker. She's carting the body away. Just chill and listen. See if we can find out anything." Xandie pushed away from the door and wandered down the hallway toward the milling crowd.

"Lila. I'm so sorry about this whole mess." A short, curvy woman, with long emerald-green hair with glitter sprinkled over it, rushed up, wringing her hands. "This just doesn't happen at the Academy."

Clio, one of the three heads of the Academy and a muse descendant, smothered Lila in a hug.

She stepped back and perused the baker. "Are you traumatized? We've brought in a healer. She is amazing with mind magic. If you need any help don't hesitate to use her."

"I'm fine, Clio. Just wondering what would cause such a severe enough reaction that the poor woman died."

"Poor woman, my furry tail." Another lady sidled up to Lila. "Britney Cygnus was a menace and a bully."

"Now, Chloe. I know you had issues with her while you were students at the Academy. But poor Ms. Cygnus has died. Can't you let your enmity go?"

"She tortured me throughout my entire schooling life. Made me miserable. Trust me, I won't forget that." The woman stood with arms crossed, glaring at the muse.

Lila stepped forward to defuse the situation. "Sylvis, right?"

"Chloe." The woman took a shuddering breath. "Sorry, the subject of that she-beast winds me up."

Lila nodded to the muse that she'd deal with the worked-up woman then maneuvered Chloe to a relatively quiet corner of the room. "She-beast being the late Britney?"

"She made my life hell during our Academy years and wasn't much better once we were grown up." Chloe dragged in a shuddering breath. "You attended the Academy, right?"

Lila nodded.

"You know what it was like. Take all the feuds and issues from the town and magnify for school. My family and hers do *not* get on. She made it her mission to torment me every chance she got." Chloe grimaced. "It didn't help that I love science. I had to tutor her for science one year and it didn't end well."

"So, I guess you hated her?" *Suspect number one?*

Chloe nodded and her nose twitched. "Oh yeah. I hated her all right, but not enough to kill. If that's what you're getting at?"

"As far as I know she died from an allergic reaction to something. I'm just interested, is all."

"A Harrow casually interested in someone, while a body lies cooling next door, screams murder suspect to me." The bunny shifter crossed her arms over her chest. "Besides, if you're scrounging for suspects, you won't have to look far. She upset a lot of people, including your grandmother and that sweaty little bald man hovering next to the bathroom." Chloe jerked her head in his direction. "I saw the two of them arguing only this morning. I couldn't hear what they said, but I thought it weird because he definitely isn't the type she'd make friends with."

Shelving the idea of interrogating the little bald man until later, Lila focused on the most concerning point the shifter had brought up. *Elspeth.* "What does the dead swan shifter have to do with my grandmother?"

"She's the reason Ms. Harrow couldn't attend this year. Apparently, there was a verbal fight last year over the bake sale best stall trophy. Then Elspeth cursed Britney with a face full of volcano-sized pimples. The shifter didn't leave the house for weeks until it cleared. I look up to your grandmother," Chloe snickered.

"Elspeth's unique all right. Britney was the head of the P.T.A. She must have kids who go here, right?"

"That's the other issue that annoyed Elspeth. Britney's son graduated last year. Her second-in-command should have taken the position over when Britney's son left."

"Who's the runner-up?"

"I am." Chloe glared at Lila. "Yes. I know how

that sounds, but again, I didn't kill her. I'm just enjoying the fallout. If you excuse me, I have better things to do with my time than be interrogated by a Harrow." The shifter stomped away from Lila.

"Attitude much?"

"Welcome to Point Muse Academy. Wasn't it like this in the dark ages when you were at school?" Es Penne popped up next to Lila.

Jerking at her sudden appearance, Lila poked a finger at the teenager. "You should have a bell around your neck. I'm old, remember the dark ages? I could have a heart attack."

"You'll live forever just to annoy Elspeth."

"Point. Is that kind of parental attitude normal around here now?"

Es shrugged, her long black hair flowing neatly over one shoulder. She blew her bangs out of the way and regarded Lila seriously for a moment. "You're thinking murder, then?"

Did everyone here have murder on the brain today? "All I know is that the bullying head of the P.T.A. died when on a school tour while one of her bullied victims watched on. I just like to get more of a picture of the swan shifter and her school-related relationships."

"Here's the download. Cygnus and Sylvis hated

each other. Their kids took after their parents and tormented each other until the Cygnus son, Peter, graduated. Now Marion Sylvis is head mean girl. Apparently, the two families have a feud going back decades."

"Why doesn't the school step in and stop the fighting?"

Es snickered. "Our head mistresses tend to float through the angst and look good while doing it. Plus, both families have always contributed heavily to the school funds. The only family that normally donates more is the Winchesters. Are we good now? I have to go spread teenage apathy amongst the crowd."

Lila waved off her sometimes-bakery minion. "Go forth and spread apathetic teenager vibes."

So, the swan and the bunny hated each other. And Elspeth had a set-to with the dead woman. Seemed about normal for Point Muse.

"I'm starting to think I need to cut my vacation short." Edie Winchester moved toward Lila.

"No Emmaline in tow?"

"Mildred turned up and has wheelchair duty, thankfully. She's in fine form today. Probably watching that horrible woman die. Too much excitement for her." Edie hunched over.

"Doesn't seem like that poor woman was well

liked." Lila glanced around the crowded hallway. "The chief of police is working through the interviews and won't get to us for a while. You want some fresh air?"

Edie brightened. "That would be great. I need to check on my snake enclosure and I want to have a chat with you about something."

Lila swept Edie a formal bow. "Lead on, green witch."

Smirking, Edie pushed through the crowd to an exit door.

"For someone new to the town, you seem to know your way around the Academy."

Leading Lila away from the school buildings, Edie headed toward the back of the school and a large, fenced enclosure with various outbuildings. "Emmaline won't let me keep my snakes on her grounds. I approached the school, and as long as I look after my snakes and allow the teachers access, they're happy. I'm here a lot." Edie unlocked the enclosure and waved Lila through.

"You said you needed to talk to me?" The quicker she got Edie talking the less time she'd have near the reptiles. Lila wasn't terrified of snakes, but she wasn't a fan of scales and fangs either.

Shifting from foot to foot, Edie nibbled on her lip

before taking a deep breath. "The way that woman died. I don't think it was an accident."

"What makes you say that?" And why did Lila feel like Point Muse was about to deliver her a side of murder...*again?*

"I'm a green witch, but I've always loved snakes. Any kind of reptile and I'm immune to venom. Snakes even come when I call. I've done a lot of research into their biology, habitat, feeding patterns and side effects of venom, et cetera."

"And?" *Here comes the boom...*

"And that woman looked like she died of a very potent snake venom. One that may have been bolstered by magic. The smoking skin is a normal reaction, but the respiratory failure, and paralysis, looked like it was caused by a neurotoxin similar to that of a snake venom on steroids."

And Edie housed snakes on Academy grounds.

She nodded at Lila. "I know what you're thinking. And that's why I brought you out here to check my snake enclosure. I didn't even know the woman, but I know venom and I'm worried I'll be suspect number one."

Along with a host of other people. "Let's check your snakes first, then worry."

Edie nodded and moved to the closest building.

"This building was perfect as it has power and is insulated." She pointed to three medium-sized terrariums. "I have a portable ceramic heat emitter and UV light for each terrarium to keep the heat at a certain temperature. I clean the terrarium weekly so it's almost due for cleanup now. My snakes are relatively young, so they only eat twice a week, but I like to come in daily and chat with them."

Actually, the room and snakes weren't as scary she thought they'd be. The three glass cases were filled with rocks, branches and water—and the snakes were small, not big Cobras. "How many do you have here?"

Edie stared earnestly at Lila. "I only brought my youngest and safest snakes with me. I have a garter snake, milk snake, river snake, and a red belly snake. Honestly, none are venomous. Although you wouldn't want to startle one into biting you."

"But the reaction the swan woman had was caused by venomous snake poison?"

"It indicates a strong venom boosted by magic. But I'm not an expert. I just don't want my girls to be blamed."

Lila frowned. "But if your snakes are the non-venomous ones, why would people think you had something to do with it?"

Edie snorted. "This is Point Muse. From what I can understand, before I could even defend myself, I'd be judged by the court of public gossip."

"You're right, unfortunately." Lila stared at the snake cages as another thought filtered through her brain. "How can you tell they're girls?"

"The males' tails are thicker and longer than the female. I can show you if you want?" Edie skipped toward a terrarium.

Lila held out a hand. "Thanks, but no thanks. It's probably safer to keep them where they are. Plus, I'm strictly into sugar, not snakes, but thanks for offering."

Edie nodded. "I forget not everyone gets as excited as I do over snakes."

"We need to head back so Braun can interview us." Lila moved out into the late morning sun and breathed deeply.

"Sorry about that. When snakes feel threatened, they discharge a musk that repels attackers. It's pretty strong and pungent. They aren't fans of travelling so they doused the shed pretty good when they first arrived. I've cleaned it out, but it hangs around. You don't really notice the smell until you breathe fresh air." Edie waited for Lila to leave the fenced enclosure and locked up behind her.

"Are you the only one who has a key?"

"Well, myself and the science teacher, but flexible teenagers could climb over the fence. If well motivated."

"Teenagers are never motivated."

"Excuse me? The Chief would like to interview Ms. Winchester." A small bald man stood nervously in front of Lila and Edie. The same man who'd been seen talking to the Swan shifter outside Bertie Boxwood's alchemy shop.

"Oh, that's me. I'll see you later, Lila." Edie hurried off toward the school building.

Lila followed at a slower pace.

The bald man picked up his pace until he drew level with Lila. "Ms. Harrow. You have to help me."

Lila stopped short. "Sorry?"

The man drew closer and hissed at Lila, "I need you to organize a meeting with Elspeth Harrow. She's the only one who'll understand and will actually protect me."

Always Elspeth with a finger in the cook pot. "Why?"

"Just organize a meeting. I'll tell her everything."

The man glanced around wildly, checking for witnesses to the meeting.

"And who do I say wants the meeting?" Other than a weird, scared, bald man?

"Rufus Moon. She'll know who I am." Without a backward glance, he scuttled off.

"Why is it always the crazy ones that need help from Elspeth?"

FOUR

"Why do secret meetings have to take place in the dead of night? Why can't we have a nice sunny afternoon meeting?" Lila grumped as she cuddled into her very warm hellhound puppy. The nights were starting to cool off, so the added heat of a warm-blooded hellhound came in handy.

"At least this time we don't need to use Great-Aunt Rose's finger to break in."

"Could you two gabbling Gertie's shut it? This is a *secret* meeting." Elspeth glared at her granddaughters. "Don't make me regret bringing you along."

Lila mimed locking her mouth and waited for Elspeth to turn away before whispering to Holly, "She only brought us in case of trouble. That way she can shove us into trouble's path and run off."

Holly giggled with a careful eye on her grandmother. "Colin would be the first to fall, he isn't made for running."

"If I had to name an Armageddon squad, he'd make it because of his radioactive belching."

"What about me? Did I make the squad? I made it, didn't I?" Holly nodded. "I made it. Good to have a Banshee with death visions on your apocalypse team."

"Ah, yes. Of course, *you* made it." Lila fist bumped Holly, but purposely kept the fact her somewhat clumsy, death obsessed cousin would be her last pick.

"Enough with your fantasy end of the world draft picks. Rufus is here." Elspeth shuffled the girls up to the back of the alchemy shop and shoved them inside as soon as Rufus opened the door.

"I wasn't expecting the whole Harrow tribe, Elspeth." The short, baldheaded man named Rufus glared at the Harrow matriarch.

Elspeth raised an eyebrow and stared Rufus down until he dropped his gaze. "The Harrows tend to be a package. Less bodies to bury that way. What did you want, Rufus?"

Lila ignored the man's complaints and wandered around the dimly lit shop with Holly mimicking her.

No one took on Elspeth and lived to talk about it. At least not in Point Muse. Lila would do some snooping while Elspeth did her intimidation thing.

Nash trotted behind Lila, his eyes faintly red. He whined and pawed the back of Lila's leg.

Lila bent down just in time to receive a wet hellhound sneeze to the face. "Yuck." Wiping away the goo, she frowned at her puppy. "You better not be getting sick, or Mom will dose you quick smart with some nasty-smelling potion."

Nash whined again, and then in a guttural tone replied with one word. "Smells."

"Oh, poor baby." Holly crouched near the puppy. "Rufus shares the shop with Bertie. Too many stinky potions in one place for a sensitive nose." She rubbed the hellhound's ears and kept away from the resulting snot missile as he sneezed again.

"Keep guard at the door, let us know if trouble comes, okay?" Lila winked at the hellhound then started rambling around the shop again, keeping an ear out for Elspeth's conversation at the same time.

"Time is money, Rufus Moon. And I'm charging you double every minute you waste mine." Elspeth flipped her long straight blond locks over her shoulder and fluffed her fake bangs.

Say what you will about Elspeth's obsessional love of brightly colored wigs, the old wicked witch rocked them. Lila drifted closer so she could hear.

On the other side of the shop, Holly did the same, both cousins ready for eavesdropping.

Rufus rubbed his hands through his non-existent hair. "It's hard. I have to respect client confidentiality, but I'm worried I'm a target."

Elspeth sighed. "Rufus, I told you your side business would cause trouble. Remember?"

"I know that. But I thought I could handle it. Plus, I've made some money." Rufus paced up and down. "But it's that stupid feud causing all the trouble." He slapped his hand down on the dusty counter. "I'm next. I know I am. You need to protect me."

"I don't need to do anything, Moon. Remember that warning I mentioned? I told you, you weren't cut out for the poison biz, and I wouldn't bail you out if you got into trouble. Especially without details of the problem."

"I can't," Rufus snapped at Elspeth before he moderated his tone, his eyes wide with his temerity.

Lila moved back hurriedly. No one barked at Elspeth if they wanted to live. She focused on the shop again. Everything looked organized, if a little dusty. At least on one side of the store. The other seemed a tad more chaotic. Bottles jumbled on shelves, tags hanging off lopsidedly or missing completely. A curtain on one side of the store stood open. The room, dimly lit from the inside, showed more of the same clutter but in an office setting. Papers coated the desk and a portion of the floor. Rufus' filing skills must exist in another dimension, since his office looked like a large trash can.

"I can't give you details yet. I have to make sure I'm right before I expose my client."

"Your funeral." Elspeth shrugged. "Can't help if I don't know the story."

"It's that Hades' cursed feud. Always landing me in trouble."

"Don't sell to both sides, and if you do...*don't get caught*." Elspeth dusted her hands off. "You want help? You got twenty-four hours before my assistance expires." She smirked at the now sweating man and pointed to her eavesdropping granddaughters. "Mush, minions. We have other fish to fry."

Lila and Holly followed Nash and Elspeth out the door.

Stomach rumbling, Holly licked her lips. "I could eat a fish fry-up."

"A figure of speech, granddaughter."

"I'm more interested in that conversation." Elspeth Harrow, the wicked witch of Point Muse, liked to operate in the shadows, but that meeting had been obscure even by her grandmother's standards.

Elspeth hmphed. "About being an idiot. I warned him. He wasn't cut out for the business, but he thought he saw dollar signs."

"And?" Holly joined the conversation and prodded Elspeth.

"Rufus deals in poisons, the more unusual, the better. He particularly likes to play with different types of snake venom. Sadly, his favorite customers are two warring clans. Feuds are bad juju. They always end in trouble and a body count."

The Sylvis and Cygnus families? "And he thinks he might be a target now?"

"*Hecate knows.* Rufus has always been a big fish in his mind, maybe he's just overestimating his own importance."

"But what if he really is a target?"

Elspeth cackled and the light from the streetlamps along Main Street extinguished with a pop. "Then good old Rufus will come crawling back to me for my help." She rubbed her hands together. "I can see a price hike in my future."

Lila didn't have to be psychic to foresee Elspeth caused mayhem in their future.

Lila yawned behind her hand. "Seriously, how long do we have to hang around this morning?"

"Until Elspeth releases us from our punishment duty."

"But we don't have to judge until the bake sale and that isn't for a few days at least. So why do I have to show up now?"

Winifred glared at her niece. "Because you and your cousin Xandie are representing the Harrow family. Stop whining. Your poor mother is the one who has to look after your sneezing hellhound. She should be the one complaining."

"Hey, I didn't know that alchemy shop would trigger an allergic reaction. He's a hellhound, I thought he'd be indestructible," Lila argued. "Besides, Elspeth wouldn't know if we deserted the sale. She's banned, remember?"

Xandie shook her head. "You should know better. This is Elspeth. She sees all." The Librarian looked over her shoulder. "Trust me, I bet she's watching us right now."

Winifred patted her nieces on their shoulders. "Quite right to be wary. Mother is a force of nature. A dark tempestuous storm with intermittent bouts of brain-addling lightning strikes." Their aunt beamed at the girls. "Now, go out and represent and pick me up a bargain."

Lila stomped off toward a stall featuring hats knitted in the shape of ferocious animals. She picked through the offerings until she found a black wolf with ear flaps. She slapped it on her head. "Close enough to Nash and shows that I'm representing the family." Lila forked some cash over to the stallholder.

"That's a wolf. Not a hellhound. The only similarity is the fact they're both black."

"Don't lay facts on me, Alexandra Meyers. I'm here under duress. This is as good as it gets."

"Testy much? No more late-night meetings for you."

Lila flicked her ear flaps down. "I can't hear you," Lila sang the last words, but ruined the effect with a giggle.

Xandie sighed and linked arms with Lila, dragging her around the outside of the hall. "Look, we don't have a choice. Let's just stroll around the room and buy a dodgy craft or two, then head to the cafeteria for sugary sustenance. How does that sound?" Xandie soothed her cousin.

"Like I'm being bribed for good behavior, but I'll take it." Lila stared morosely around the crowded hall. Plenty of Point Muse residents had turned out for the annual Academy yard sale. Every resident with overflowing crafty detritus had shown up with a stall. Even her Aunt Winifred had turned up with her candles and bath salts. Holly's mother had a candle and potion store in town and a habit of foisting candles on family members. Winifred sported the same amber eyes as the rest of the family, along with curves aplenty and bright red hair. She was also the nicest of all the Harrows.

"Learn anything interesting at the late-night meeting?"

"Only that Nash is allergic to alchemy, and Rufus dabbles in poisons and currently thinks he's the next victim."

Xandie stopped and stared at Lila. "Before the previous body's been designated a murder victim?"

"Odds are not in favor of accidental death."

"What have I told you about speculation, Harrow?" Matthew Grim, reaper, and Zach Braun, Xandie's boyfriend and Chief of Police, both glared at the cousins.

Xandie held a hand up. "Hey, I didn't say anything about murder. It was *her*." She pointed to Lila and shuffled closer to her bear shifter boyfriend.

"Where is the family solidarity?" Lila rolled her eyes. "Besides, it's Point Muse. Speculation tends to be based on the sad fact we're the murder capital of the supernatural world."

Grim flipped one of Lila's wolf ear flaps. "New fashion trend?"

"It's a hellhound, not a wolf." Lila slapped the reaper's hand away. "Now, can we get back to whether or not Britney 'mean girl' Cygnus was bumped off?"

Braun ran a hand through sandy brown hair. "Fine, it will get around town soon enough. Britney Cygnus was definitely murdered. The police healer confirmed the presence of a poisonous substance foreign to the science experiment."

"What kind poison?"

"Some kind of supercharged snake venom. That's all we know so far until more test results come in."

"Murder, what a surprise," Lila cackled in a poor imitation of Elspeth.

Braun pointed a warning finger at Lila and Xandie. "We all know you Harrows can't help yourself when it comes to murder, but this time, you need to watch yourself. The poison used to kill the victim is particularly nasty. It stripped the top layer of skin off her arm and face and seared her lungs. Stay out of trouble when you poke your noses into my business."

"Emphasis on when." Matthew smirked at Lila. "Is it a good time to tell you I moved your office around?"

"*What*," Lila exploded, bouncing on the balls of the feet like a prizefighter. "No freeloader should touch a baker's special stuff. It's like a rule." Nasty stuff-moving reaper. It was always the cute, quiet ones you had to watch out for.

Matthew leaned in closer, his breath tickling her skin and sending shivers down her spine.

"I even color-coded your pens," he whispered.

Focusing on his words and not her reaction, Lila launched herself at Grim, hands extended. "Why, you pen obsessed..."

Xandie snagged her cousin and swung her away from the organizing torturer. "Calm down, drama lama. He's just trying to get a rise out of you."

"I'll give him..." Her words were drowned out by the sudden high-pitched babbling behind them. Confused, Lila swung around and faced a suddenly surging crowd. She ducked as a fuchsia satin dress soared over her head.

"I want my money back. Your goods are infected."

"Excuse me? My fashion wares are completely clean and ethically sourced. Which is more than I can say about you."

Lila exchanged a glance with Xandie. This kind of mayhem normally had an Elspeth Harrow behind it. Heading for the warring yard sale attendees, Lila pulled up short and stared. "What has happened to you, Delia?"

A middle-aged woman with platinum blonde hair glared at the stall owner standing behind a table piled with dresses. "She happened. I bought one of her diseased prom dresses and slipped it over my head to make sure of the fit. Next thing I know I'm covered in purple dots. She's selling diseased formal wear. It should be against the law."

"Why, I never," the gray-rinse elderly lady behind the stall gasped in outrage. "Don't blame me for your bad bathing habits. If you washed regularly, rashes wouldn't happen."

Before anyone could retaliate, another woman with a lavender pixie cut and a matching set of purple polka dots threw another satin number on the table.

Several other colorful, irate women crowded in, shaking dresses in the air.

"This definitely feels like an Elspeth hit." Lila stepped out of the way of a purple-spotted matron.

"Except there's no way Elspeth got through the door. She's banned, remember? And the Muses are all on Elspeth duty. No way she slipped in."

"This is Elspeth. The mayhem magnet. The chaos lover. Trust me, she's here somewhere." Lila motioned Braun and Grim forward and raised her voice. "Ladies. Chief Braun is here to personally sort out your issues."

The crowd surged forward toward the chief and Lila stepped back with a victorious got-you smile.

"Who knew Point Muse could be so exciting? Puts a whole new spin on paint the town purple." The same perky cheerleader, with bouncy blonde hair and a fluffy orange kitten draped over a shoulder, popped up next to Lila, munching on a bag of popcorn.

"Isn't it paint the town red?" Lila frowned as the smirking teenager flicked a lock of hair over her shoulder, hitting the kitten in the face. The feline spat out a mouthful of hair, gagging. Lila frowned.

Something about that too energetic teenager niggled at her sleuthing nerve. *Something familiar.*

"Whatever. Still entertaining to watch. Ta ta, losers." The cheerleader threw popcorn at the Harrows, and then skipped off.

Something stunk in the town of Point Muse...

FIVE

"Is he still there?"

Lila poked her head around the doorway and peered out. "Looks like he's given up. There's no sign of him."

Xandie stepped into the hallway. "This is all your fault, Lila Harrow."

"How could I know he'd try on one of the dresses to prove it wasn't infected. I 'm not psychic."

"Now he has purple spots all over and he's out for Harrow blood."

"Good thing you're a Meyers then."

Xandie bit her lip but couldn't control the laughter bubbling out. "Did you see his face? Grim's too. So funny. Shame Elspeth couldn't see her handiwork. "

"Have you come over to my side? You think she hexed the prom dress stall?"

Xandie stared at her cousin. "A week-long celebration she's been banned from, a stall featuring pre-loved formal dresses from decades of the Academy dances. What's to resist? Of course she hexed the stall. It's just hilarious Braun and Grim got caught in her purple polka dot mayhem."

"Ah, stray Harrows." A tall willowy muse with bright blue hair eyed the duo. "Since we're still dealing with the drama of the yard sale, we have instituted school tours. Esmeralda is currently leading one nearby." The woman pinned a stern gaze on the girls. "I expect to see you join her." Then she swished off with a twirl of her flowing dress.

"I take it that means a command performance. No way out," Lila muttered.

"Some of the crowd ratted out your hiding spot. Since they're trying to fix the spot issue, we're all under school tour arrest. No chance of time off for good behavior." Es Penne strode toward Lila, a dark thundercloud expression gracing her face. Edie and Emmaline Winchester, and Mildred, the house-keeper, trailed behind.

"Looks like someone else isn't too happy about conducting a tour," Xandie whispered to Lila.

"What was your first clue, Librarian?" The dragon teenager pointed to Emmaline with a silvery claw. "Line up behind the grand dame of sour. All hands and feet in, this could be a bumpy ride." Without bothering to check if Lila and Xandie followed her directions, Es stomped off.

"I don't think she's any more impressed to be leading the tour than we, or Mildred for that matter, are to take it." Xandie pointed to the dour housekeeper.

"That could be her default face."

Es raised her voice and spoke over Lila. "If you could just step to the side of this hallway, you will see the first of our display cases honoring previous alumni." The dragon tapped on the glass. "The first display case features the graduating classes of nineteen forty-eight and forty-nine. Enjoy the display of oldie fashion."

The teenager moved out of the way and leaned against the wall, picking at a claw.

Edie crowded in and peered at the photos. "Wow, check out the clothing."

Lila and Holly peeped over Edie's shoulder. "Plaid skirt, sweater, white socks and loafers. Trend-setters," Lila snickered until a sharp jab to her rib cage had her hissing, "Hecate's toenails."

She spun and eyeballed Emmaline Winchester in her wheelchair just behind her.

"Making fun of your elders is not an admirable trait, Lila Harrow. But I suppose you get that from your grandmother." Emmaline glared at Lila.

"I..."

A squeal of excitement erupting from Edie saved Lila from an inappropriate reply.

"Emmaline. I found you in the gardening club photo." She tapped the glass.

Except for the dull red hair and the absence of a wheelchair, teenage Emmaline looked a lot like elderly Emmaline. Same sour face. Most of the group in the photo stood to one side away from the sullen teenage green witch. Winchester hadn't been much of a joiner even back then.

"Look at all the ribbons the club won. They were talented." Edie smiled at her great-aunt. "I bet since you're a green witch you were an amazing green thumb."

"None of those ribbons were mine. My talents were never appreciated," Emmaline spat the words out, hate blazing out from her fierce eyes. "They were shortsighted, never could see my genius."

Edie gaped at her great-aunt.

Lila butted in before Emmaline could vocally eviscerate her great-niece.

"Where's Elspeth? Isn't she the same age as you?"

"I don't see her anywhere." Xandie scanned the photos. "Nothing."

"Elspeth Harrow had already graduated from the Academy quite a bit before I did." Emmaline sniffed, her ire at the gardening club forgotten.

"I thought she was around your age?" Then again, Elspeth had fought in World War two so that would make her older than Emmaline, but how much older?

"Elspeth Harrow lies. Something to remember, niece, when you deal with the Harrows. They'd bend things to suit themselves." Emmaline slapped Mildred's hand away. "Onward. This tour tires me."

"You aren't the only one," Es muttered and pushed off from the wall. "If you care to follow me? As we pass through the alumni hallway, you will see various graduating classes. Most of the families have stuck around in town. Pity for them." She walked a few meters down the hallway and flapped a hand. "Go forth and laugh at past generations."

"I don't think she's really getting into her role as a tour guide."

Lila snorted at Xandie's words. "I think we should be happy she hasn't set fire to the photos yet."

"It's really interesting from a historical standpoint, looking at all these photos. It's a shame Emmaline wasn't in any more of them."

"I get the feeling, Edie, your Great-Aunt preferred to lurk in the background." Lila strolled along the hallway of photos and paused next to Emmaline. She leaned in and peered at a photo. "Cygnus, that's the name of the swan shifter who just died?"

"Britney Cygnus, the jewel of the Cygnus clan." Emmaline huffed.

"Why am I not surprised she was a cheerleader?"

Emmaline tapped a yellowed nail on the photo display case. "Head cheerleader to be exact and closely nipping at her manicured toes, Chloe Sylvis."

"Rivals back then too?"

"Before they were even born. Their families have feuded for generations. Cygnus and Sylvis, bound to hate as each generation are born." Emmaline adjusted the blanket draped over her legs. "The feud has drawn blood, financial ruin, and even death over the generations. But that bear shifter boyfriend of your cousin and his family have managed to curtail the most distasteful results of the feuding... At least until now."

"Britney Cygnus." Had Chloe hated the mean girl enough to follow family tradition and remove her permanently?

"Indeed." Emmaline crooked a finger at Lila.

Leaning in, Lila fought a sneeze that built, triggered by the strong stench of lavender and stale body odor.

"Back in the distant day, both families had a certain reputation in the use of toxic substances." Emmaline tapped the side of her nose. "Just between us, of course." She nodded to the ever-lurking Mildred, who spun the wheelchair, narrowly missing Lila's foot, and pushed her charge down the hallway.

"Toxic substances equal code for poison."

"Talking to yourself about poisons isn't a good sign. I thought the witchy baker was staying out of the investigation?" Xandie quirked an eyebrow at her cousin.

"I can't help it if clues fall in my lap. What am I supposed to do?"

"Ignore them?" Xandie and Lila looked at each other for a moment and then burst into laughter.

"Inside joke?" Edie stared, confused, at the women.

"Just our inability to restrain our curiosity. It's a Harrow flaw." Lila linked arms with Edie. "I think our tour guide has had enough. Maybe we should join her before she explodes into righteous dragon fury and eviscerates us with her claws."

Es stepped forward and rolled her eyes. "You're such a drama witch. I'd rather flame than eviscerate. Now if you could just keep up, we can end this farce." Ignoring the titters behind her, the dragon led the group back to the hall and the yard sale stalls.

"Do you think Braun's still hunting us?" Xandie peered around Lila, using her as camouflage.

"I think he's found you already." Matthew Grim loomed over the women, glaring. His gaze centered on Lila.

She braced herself. The reaper's steely gray eyes bored into her, but he seemed remarkably polka dot free. Lila decided to prod him. "Where is that lovely shade of purple you were wearing? It really lifted your complexion."

"Now, Lila, dear. There's no need to be petty." Winifred bopped Lila on the nose. "As for that nasty spot issue that no one can trace back to the Harrows, I had enough potions on hand for a makeshift remedy." Winifred glared at Lila and Xandie meaningfully.

"How lucky was that?" The teenager in her cheerleader costume wandered up with her somewhat pudgy ginger kitten following close behind her. The girl smirked and twirled her long, blond ponytail. The kitten wandered over and rubbed against the girl's legs. The feline stood for a moment, staring up at Edie, then meandered off with a shake of its body.

Lila covered her mouth and nose as a pungent tuna odor wafted past. An odd idea wiggled into the dark recesses of Lila Harrow's mind. She turned to the cheerleader. "Isn't it odd that my aunt had exactly the right ingredients needed to remove the spots. Almost serendipitous like someone had planned it."

The cheerleader nodded, her cornflower blue eyes wide. "I know, right? I guess everyone is just plain lucky all-round."

"Ah-huh." And all Harrows were innocent and pure. Elspeth mayhem was afoot. Lila pointed to a small basket the girl carried with blue iced cookies. "Cookies for the yard sale masses. Or just a fashion accessory?"

The teenager smirked. "One of the old girls who run the school told me to hand them out. Soothe the crowd with sugar and all that. Want one?" The blonde held a cookie out, a smirk in place and a wicked glint in her eye reminiscent of Elspeth Harrow.

"You know what? Think I'll pass. Might be safer."

"I'll have one. I haven't had a sugar hit today." Xandie reached around Lila and grabbed a cookie.

"I wouldn't do that…" Lila gave up as Xandie inhaled the cookie and reached for another. "Too late. Enjoy the mayhem." Lila distanced herself from her cookie-munching cousin and whispered to her aunt, "I hope you bought a heap of potions. You're going to need it."

Winifred looked worried for a moment. "Do we have an Elspeth-related issue?"

Lila winked. "Let's just say I'd stay away from those cookies Xandie's munching on." She shook her head and wandered off before the mayhem started. *Honestly, you'd have thought her cousin would have learned by now.* "Never take a freebie, there could be Elspeth strings attached."

"Is there a reason why you're hot footing it away from your normally glued to your side cousin?" Matthew moved up next to Lila and matched his stride to hers as they strolled around the room.

"Nope. Just perusing the wares." Lila pointed to

the store with knitted sweaters for garden gnomes. "That would make a great present for your mom."

"Stop distracting me, but you're right. Both my mother and my father would love it." Grim slid an arm around Lila's waist and directed her to a relatively quiet corner of the hall. "Why is the rat deserting the sinking ship?"

Lila tried to block the feel of the reaper's heavy arm around her waist and opted for the distraction of righteous fury. "How dare you call me a rat." She stepped away from the reaper's warmth and glared at the too-perceptive man.

"Not a rat. Just a Harrow making sure she's out of the chaos zone. What's going on? Is this about the body?"

That was her cue to distract Matthew from the impending Harrow-caused mayhem. "Yes. You got me. I'm worried about more bodies turning up." Lila looked down at her feet and practiced a concerned, worried face.

Matthew rubbed Lila's back. "You don't have to worry about anything. Braun has it handled, and he's called me in to consult. Grim Inc has dealt with hundreds of different kinds of death, and I have my dad going through the database. We're on top of it."

"That sounds very comforting." Lila peeked out of the corner of her eyes at the crowd building near where Xandie and the cheerleader had stood. She shuffled a few steps toward the exit. Matthew followed her.

Matthew's brow furrowed as he stared at Lila. "Since when have you been concerned about more bodies and when have you ever been happy for Braun to take over?" He pointed a finger menacingly at Lila. "What have you got planned?"

Before Lila could respond, a high-pitched meow, followed by a squeal of *Geronimo*, sounded throughout the room as the teenager and her tuna-scented feline bolted for a side door.

Xandie fought through the crowd and stood on a chair. She pointed directly at her cousin. "Lila Marie Harrow..." Xandie's last word dissolved into the strident squawking of a duck. The Librarian coughed into her fist and tried again, but more furious squeaks and squawks exploded out of her mouth.

Matthew stared gob-smacked at the Librarian balancing on a chair and screaming duck obscenities at her cousin.

"Time to go, Reaper, before the Librarian or her bear shifter boyfriend catch up with us. It's every person for themselves." Lila grabbed the reaper's hand and dragged him out of the hall.

"Tell me you didn't cause that?"

"Do I look like Elspeth?"

"But she's banned."

Lila snorted. "When has that ever stopped my grandmother? She's hanging around all right, under everyone's noses." Lila sidestepped the pink-haired muse who'd stopped to stare at the milling crowd as the cacophony of barnyard noises filled the room.

"The way I see it, Grim, you have two choices."

Matthew allowed Lila to tow him away from the hall. "What choices would those be?"

"Stay and deal with the barnyard cleanup or a road trip in my bakery van." Lila dropped his arm and headed outside to the car park.

"Ta da." She swept her arm in a majestic wave at her iridescent blue van. Nash, her hellhound pet, sat in the driver's seat with his snout pushed through the partially opened window.

"Why do I think both choices threaten my life and sanity?"

"Because you ain't stupid?" Lila winked and hopped into her van after persuading Nash to give up his place in the front seat of the vehicle. Then she revved the engine and waited for the reaper to join her. She just hoped Matthew was wrong. Because she needed answers, not issues. Between Elspeth's malevolent meddling and Britney's body, she was afraid the situation would spin out of control.

And in Point Muse that meant a body count.

SIX

"Tell me again why l allowed you to run us out of town in your deathtrap of a van?" Matthew groaned and stretched his body.

The reaper's shirt rode up his stomach an inch, exposing pale skin and sculpted muscle. Lila tore her eyes away. *Stop staring, Lila. So what if the reaper has a tight stomach?*

Nash jumped down and tangled in Lila's feet, distracting her from her reaper appreciation. "Calm down, boy."

"He's just glad we arrived in one piece."

"Enough whining. We're still within Point Muse boundaries. The whole ride took ten minutes."

"Ten bone-jarring minutes of my life I'll never get back." Matthew crouched next to Nash and scratched the hellhound's ears. "Why are we here, other than you wanted to torment me with your lack of driving skills?"

Lila shrugged. "Hey, be grateful. There's only a few Harrows who drive. Most of us are mayhem incarnate behind the wheel. Something to do with our weird witchy gifts. We think it interferes with our driving."

"Stop stalling. Why are we here?"

Lila blew a breath out. "This monument to lack of taste and too much money is the Cygnus family compound." The gray stone house with multiple turrets, wide sweeping stairs and a very stable, metal gate, looked like it would fit into the English country-side, rather than the Maine coast.

"Britney's family?" Matthew stood and dusted off his trousers. "You know Braun's already inter-viewed them? Why do you need to?"

"Britney and Chloe hated each other. I want to know how far each family would go to get revenge." Lila tapped the intercom. "Lila Harrow and Matthew Grim, Reaper. Here to ask some follow-up questions."

The intercom burst into an audible spray of white noise before falling silent.

"They'll never let you or Nash in. Braun had to

push to get them to talk to him and he's law enforcement."

"Ye of little faith." Lila winked as the gates opened with a groan. "You'd be surprised what doors the fear of Elspeth will open."

With Nash keeping close, Lila stomped up the stone stairs and rang the doorbell.

The door creaked open and a decidedly decrepit old man in an immaculate black suit waved them inside. "Madam Cygnus is in the library. Your hound can wait here."

Nash growled and red flickered for a moment in his eyes.

Lila shook her head. "No dice, old man. The hellhound stays with me."

The butler sniffed. "If you wish, but I refuse to clean up after a puppy." He directed the trio to the library with a wave of his hand.

"Told you so. Everyone's too scared of Elspeth to not let us, including our hellhound, in," Lila whispered.

"No one wants to cross the wicked witch of Point Muse." Madam Cygnus rose from her chair next to a table covered in papers. "Please, take a seat, Ms. Harrow."

Lila winked at the butler, who slammed the library's door closed in response.

Nash settled against Lila's feet, his eyes tracking the swan shifter's every move.

"You have to excuse Mason. He and my grand-daughter Britney were very close." The skin over the shifter's cheekbones grew parchment white and lines bracketed the woman's mouth.

"I'm sorry for your loss." Lila gestured to the reaper. "This is Matthew Grim. I'm not sure if you've heard, but Grim Inc has set up an office in Point Muse."

Matthew offered a hand to the grieving shifter. The older woman clasped his hand gingerly before she let go. He cleared his throat. "I want to assure you, Madam, Britney has moved on and doesn't suffer. I dealt with her myself."

The swan matriarch's face twisted for a moment. She settled back into her chair, her grief hidden behind a social mask again. "You can call me Bettina. Thank you for your kind words. The Cygnus clan is grateful to know Britney has moved on to a better place."

"Could you please pass on our sympathies to Britney's parents." Lila made a point of frowning. "I assumed they would be here."

Bettina smiled in a practiced move. "My daughter and son-in-law are on a business trip. They've been notified and are making their way back. It's better they are away for the moment until calmer heads can prevail."

"Does the clan blame the school for Britney's death? I'm only new to town, but the Academy seemed very competent and devastated over your granddaughter's loss."

"The Academy is always conscientious in their every action." Bettina leaned forward, her eyes boring into Lila and Matthew, scrutinizing their reactions. "We blame others for my granddaughters' murderous demise."

Let the clan feuding beginning. "Surely Britney's death was a tragic accident?" If this was an old school mystery, Bettina's reply would be loaded with accusations and innuendos that would lead Lila to a convenient pool of suspects.

Bettina let out an elegant snort at odds with the steel-spine, gray-haired matriarch image. "Snake venom in her body doesn't say accidental to me. Someone murdered my granddaughter."

Lila cocked her head, considering the Swan. Someone should tell Braun he had a leak in his department. "And just how did you discover that Britney was killed with snake venom?"

"Wasn't hard to work out, considering her symptoms. There's only one shifter clan in town that has a reputation and no conscience when dealing with snake venom." The shifter spat one word out, "Sylvis."

Matthew interjected, "Pardon me if I'm wrong, but I had heard a rumor that your family deals in poisons as well?"

Hissing through clenched teeth, Bettina stood and paced the library floor.

Nash stiffened, and a low growl rumbled from him as he watched the woman pace.

Lila rubbed the puppy's head but focused on the shifter's rigid posture. Whatever Bettina knew, she felt very strongly about it.

"Our family through the generations have developed a knowledge and expertise in various poisons. The Sylvis clan has forced us to evolve in how we deal with toxic substances."

Okay, so both families had dabbled in poison. "What about snake venom?"

Bettina eyed Lila like she was a nasty bug underfoot. "The Cygnus clan has only ever dealt with snake venom to build up our immunity to the Sylvis poisons. That's how I know someone murdered Britney."

Finally getting to the clue bit of the conversation. "Because she had venom in her body?"

"Plain venom, even in large quantities, could not have killed my granddaughter because of her immunity. We start training our children's systems from birth. But Lamia venom would have, and that means the Sylvis clan." Bettina closed her hands into fists, every inch of her body vibrating rage. "Those murderers disguised as a family have stalked my clan for generations. More than one accidental sickness or death has occurred since both clans settled in Point Muse."

Lila cleared her throat. "No offence. But Britney didn't have the best of reputations in town."

"Britney was a strong-willed woman and made enemies because of it. But the Sylvis calling card is Lamia venom. They have access to other venoms as well and even keep their own snakes." Bettina shuddered. "The more civilized of us import our venom."

Poison didn't equal civilized in Lila's book. "Where do you get your venom from?"

"I suppose you'll find out easily enough from Elspeth. We buy from Rufus Moon. He supplies both clans with certain substances. But as I mentioned, those Sylvis degenerates milk their own venom from captive snakes."

"And the Lamia?" Matthew added his own question. "Where do they get the Lamia venom from? I was under the impression it's very rare."

Bettina sneered. "I'm not the police or a nosy Harrow. Surely you can do your own research?"

Nash growled low and soft at the shifter.

Lila stood. "Never mind, Nash. We'll just go and interview the other half of the feud. The Sylvis clan. I'm sure they will be just as forthcoming as the Cygnus family."

"Do what you wish, Harrow. But bear in mind, every word out of those rabbits' mouths is a lie." Bettina turned her back on Lila and Matthew and stared out the window.

"Thank you for speaking to us, Bettina. Again, sympathies on your loss." Matthew shepherded Lila to the library door.

"Just one more question." Lila popped her head around Matthew. "You mentioned Britney had enemies?"

Bettina answered without turning to face Lila. "Chloe Sylvis, of course. I know someone observed my granddaughter arguing with Rufus. And she and

Emmaline Winchester had butted heads as well, about projects concerning the Academy."

"Thanks, Bettina." *A few names to start with at least.*

"Shut the door on your way out."

Matthew yanked Lila out of the library and closed the door softly behind them. "She just lost her granddaughter. You could have been gentler in your questioning."

Lila snorted. "First of all, I'm a Harrow, subtlety is not my middle name. Second, that woman is more worried about planning revenge than grieving her granddaughter's death. I'm sure she'll ignore my inelegant interview technique." Reaching out, Lila patted Matthew's stubbled cheek. "You're *so* sweet and innocent. It's almost a crime to corrupt you." She moved her hand away and rubbed her palm on her jeans, trying to erase the feel of the man's skin.

"The front door is this way." The butler jerked the door open.

"Let's skedaddle and blow this joint."

"Spending too much time with Colin and Elspeth?"

Lila acknowledged Matthew's words with a sneer. Truth be told, Colin, Elspeth's talking pug, had a way with words that a hard-boiled noir detective would love. Sometimes a Harrow's words just needed extra drama.

The butler sniffed as Lila and Matthew stepped onto the sweeping front steps. "I hope your hound controlled himself. The matriarch is very particular about the cleanliness of her house."

What a ...

Nash strutted up to the door and carefully lifted his leg a few inches, leaving behind a smoking puddle on the doorstep.

The butler swore and leapt back.

Lila smirked. "Hellhounds have feelings too."

Nash trotted over to Lila's side and skipped down the stairs toward a waiting Matthew.

"Was that really necessary?" Matthew muttered.

"Nash clean," the hound grumbled in a low, rough tone.

"See?" Lila pointed at her puppy. "Nash seemed to think it was."

The trio slipped through the heavy metal gate as it slid closed behind them.

"I think you made an enemy back there."

Lila hopped into her neon van and gunned the engine. "The butler or the vengeful Madam Cygnus?"

"Both." Matthew strapped himself in and Nash

settled on the floor between the two seats. "Promise me we'll make it back to Point Muse in one piece?"

"My grandmother always says you should never make a promise you can't keep." She spun the wheel and planted a foot down, churning rocks under the van's wheels as she sped back onto the road. Poor Reaper, Lila shouldn't tease, but his reactions were priceless.

The Cygnus clan lived in another compound on the other side of town. A scenic coastal drive on a clear day, but this afternoon was dingy, and a thick fog already rolled in off the ocean.

A low rumble from next to her seat derailed Lila's inner travel monologue.

"Lila? I think we have an issue," Matthew's voice cracked.

Taking a chance, Lila quickly glanced at Nash. His eyes flared red, and his growl increased in tempo. She concentrated back on the road. "Speak to me, Matthew. I can't take my eyes off the road, or we'll end up in pieces."

Nash leapt to his feet, his large shoulders wedged between the driver and passenger seats. He let out a sharp yip and Matthew swore.

"Argh." Matthew's manly yell reached girlish

frequencies. He slapped at his seat and wrenched out his scythe, swatting the air with it.

"Have you lost your marbles?"

"Pull over, Lila. We have a big issue." Matthew fought to keep his voice even.

"No can do, freaky reaper. The road opens up just down here and then I can pull over."

Lila frowned as something green flickered on the very edge of her peripheral vision. "Speak to me. What's the issue?"

Nash opened his mouth and burped. A ribbon of flame shot out and covered a green and brown smudge between the van's seats.

"What the heck-a-doodle was that?"

"The reason you need to pull over." Matthew chopped with his scythe and a rotten musky smell filled the interior of the van, along with the odor of burnt meat.

Lila pulled the van off the road as fast as she could. She turned in her seat only to find Matthew had already bolted from the van. "Rats leave a sinking ship, why not reapers?" Lila yelled out the passenger door.

Matthew pointed with his now extended scythe "Get out of the van. Now, Lila."

His freaked-out voice forced Lila into action.

With a sigh, she released her seatbelt and opened the door. Just as she hopped out, something dropped onto the seat she'd recently vacated.

Nash leapt up and grabbed it in his mouth, shaking his head from side to side. Smoke trickled from his nose.

Lila backed away and bumped into Matthew. She raised a shaking finger and pointed at the van. "Someone defiled my van of sugary goodness with creepy reptiles." Lila laid her head back and wailed like her Banshee cousin.

Matthew patted Lila's shoulder. "I think your puppy has it sorted."

The van rocked as Nash pounced, flamed, and shredded the wriggling snakes. After five minutes, a loud burp sounded from the van's interior and smoke drifted out of the open doors. Nash tumbled down onto the ground through the open driver's door and collapsed in a heap, his stomach bulging and a dopey, doggy grin on his face.

"Nash? You okay?" Lila stepped up to her dog and poked his swollen stomach.

The puppy groaned and let out another burp, accompanied by a fried meat scented blast of hot breath. "Gone," the hound grumbled in his gravelly voice.

"Looks like he enjoyed the snack. I think we're good to get back on the road again. I need to get to the bakery and fumigate snake stink from my van before I do anything else."

Matthew shrunk his scythe back to pen size and stashed it away in his pocket. "I think your first move when we get back home is to work out just who wanted to hurt you."

Lila squashed the trickle of warmth caused by his use of the word home. The reaper was right, though. Someone tried to hurt her with snakes. If Nash hadn't craved fried snake, they were close enough to the coastline she could have driven straight off the road. Neither reaper nor baker would have survived the fall to the beach below.

A Harrow held a grudge like nobody's witch. And death by snake was something Lila would neither forgive nor forget.

"Someone just made a big mistake."

SEVEN

"Is this really necessary?" Chloe Sylvis tapped blush-pink short nails on the door to her heated snake enclosure. "I assure you all my snakes are accounted for. Is this because of something that old swan harridan said? I wouldn't believe her, every word she utters is a lie."

"Funny, she said the same thing about you." Lila glared and crossed arms over her chest. As soon as she arrived home, Grim had called Braun and reported the snake incident. The Chief's crime scene team swarmed her van. At least they'd cleaned and fumigated as they went. Her pretty bakery van was now back to its normal snake-free self.

"Ah, mom?" A skinny, teenage blonde girl stood in the heated enclosure nibbling on a nail.

Chloe shook her head. "Not now, Marion. Chief Braun and the nosy Harrow need to poke around my snakes."

"That's the thing."

Chief Braun frowned at the teenage bunny shifter. "Is there an issue, Marion? Something we need to know?"

"Marion," Chloe warned her daughter. "Is this important?"

"Geez, let the poor girl talk." Lila rolled her eyes. How was the girl expected to answer if everyone talked over her?

"Thanks for the help, Ms. Harrow." Marion's lips curved as she took in Lila's plain shirt and jeans. She turned her attention to her mother. "Some of the snakes got out. I can't find them anywhere."

"What?" Chloe shrieked, shoved her daughter aside, then ran into the enclosure.

Braun followed the shifter inside.

Marion leaned against the building and picked at a nail. "I don't know what the drama is. A few snakes are missing. So what?"

The joy of teenage apathy. "Snakes were roaming wild in my van. There could have been a nasty accident."

The teenager rolled her eyes. "Please, they're

common garden snakes. Only an idiot would be scared of them. Besides, we aren't the only ones who keep snakes in town."

"Details?"

"The niece of that wheelchair witch. She keeps snakes at school. All different kinds of snakes."

Edie Winchester. Lila nodded thoughtfully. "She's already checked hers a few days ago."

"That was a few days ago. Who knows what could have happened by now? Always blame the bunny."

"Why would Edie bother to plant snakes in my car? She's barely got a connection to the school or the town."

Shrugging, Marion scrutinized Lila. "She's a Winchester. Just like those Swan shifters, they always worm their way into Academy business. I mean, that swan who died? Her kid had already left school. Why stay on as head of the P.T.A.?"

Marion Sylvis was sulky and self-centered, but she wasn't wrong. "The Cygnus matriarch told us that your family shoots snake venom and has a certain reputation with removing competitors with poison."

Marion snickered. "Shoots venom? Makes us

sound like addicts. We build our immunity gradually, that's all. Not against the law."

"And removing competition with poison?"

"The bunnies and the swans have been at each other's throats since Point Muse was founded. Both our families have graveyards in the closet," Marion said. "Doesn't mean we killed the swan woman."

"But a little birdie told me Britney Cygnus died of Lamia venom. Know anything about that?"

Teenage sullenness dropped away to be replaced with confusion. Meaning little bunny shifter had no clue Britney had been murdered. *Interesting...*

"Seriously?" Marion's voice squeaked. She took a quick look over her shoulder before heading around the corner of the enclosure.

Lila followed, keeping an eye on the teenager in case she shifted and became predator bunny.

"Look, our families hate each other," Marion admitted. "David Cygnus left school last year. He's the only decent swan shifter I've ever met." The teenager chewed her lip. "Don't mention anything, but he and I were...close." She blinked rapidly. "We never told our families because they'd freak."

Romeo and Juliet of the shifter world. "What does that have to do with Lamia venom?"

Marion drifted closer. "My family tries to always

stay a step ahead of the Cygnus clan. Generations ago, the family decided to diversify into poison. We supply the Alchemy shop in town with different potions. Some of them have a Lamia base. The potions are more potent that way."

Bingo. "You use Lamia venom."

"We do, but we don't farm it ourselves. There's a supplier in town. But they're anonymous. Rufus at the Alchemy shop is the go-between. He has a ledger he writes everything down in. He knows who the supplier is if you can find him. He's a sneaky kind of rat. And you didn't hear that from me, okay?"

"Isn't it illegal to question a minor without a representative present?" Chloe Sylvis stood behind Lila, arms crossed and scowl in place.

"Just shooting the breeze while you two deal with your snake issues." Lila winked at the irate bunny.

"Now, if you excuse us, we got places to be and cakes to bake." Lila linked arms with her cousin's boyfriend and dragged him away from poisonous bunny central.

"We have things to do?"

Lila patted Zach's arm. "We do, Chief Braun. I have some honey buns calling your name and we need a plan of action. War counsel at the bakery."

At the mention of honey buns, Braun's eyes gleamed, and he skipped to his patrol car.

The things sugar and honey could do to a manly bear shifter.

"I think we should stage an intervention." Holly poked Xandie's boyfriend in the shoulder. "See? He didn't even move. He's in a sugar coma."

Xandie shrugged, unconcerned. "All the Brauns are the same. Give them a pile of honey buns and their minds shut down until they process the honey. It's a species flaw."

"At least we know how to distract him if we need to." Lila winked and nodded at Hester, her bakery brownie, who'd been with the Harrow family for decades. She had a light touch with baking and could run Lila's store with one arm tied behind her back. "Even if Chief bear shifter is mindless in a sugar coma, we need to work out what we do next." Lila regarded her blank-faced cousins and the drooling police chief. "Don't talk all at once."

Holly spread her hands open and shrugged. "I got nothing. Xandie's our expert sleuth, ask her."

"I am not an expert. Bodies find me, remember?"

Xandie glared at Lila. "Drama loves you. So, it's your turn to sleuth up."

Nash whimpered under the table. His hot breath tickled Lila's legs even through her jeans. She reached a hand down and scratched one of his ears. "Marion Sylvis mentioned a ledger that Rufus kept with all his poison suppliers, stocks sold and all his clients. It might have something about who's supplying the Lamia poison and who's buying. That's our first step, hunt Rufus and his ledger down."

"I wouldn't trust anything that snooty Sylvis tells you. She has a passing grade in lying."

Es Penne, teenage dragon, stood next to Lila, a frilly pink apron tied around her waist.

Lila covered a snort of laughter with a pretend cough. "Pink really suits you, Esmeralda."

"Stuff it, Harrow." She pointed a silver claw at Lila and smoke trickled out of one nostril. "Hester made me wear it while I loaded the van up with food for the bake sale tomorrow, so I didn't mess my outfit up. I'm more afraid of her than your ridicule," Es sneered in general at the table.

"Wise choice." Lila considered the dragon. Mouthy was Es Penne's go-to attitude, but she had good instincts. "You don't think Marion told me the truth?"

"I have no clue what she said to you, but I know her. Whatever she said, it wasn't the whole story. But what do I know?" Es untied her apron and dumped it in the middle of Lila's table before stomping away.

"You trust what bully bunny said?" Xandie shoved another honeybun onto her boyfriend's plate.

"I think the ledger makes sense and we need to find it and Rufus and grill him for information."

"Grilling. My favorite form of torture. Those were the good old days." Elspeth popped up next to Lila and cackled. The bakery's lights flickered, accompanied by a buzzing noise.

The evil hag routine played havoc with her utility bill. "Cut out the theatrics, Elspeth. Unless you want to pay my bills," Lila grouched at her grandmother.

Elspeth patted her hot pink wig and fluffed the short chin-length bob. "No act, just one hundred percent pure Elspeth Harrow."

"You're definitely full of a hundred percent something," Holly muttered to her cousins.

"Careful, death girl. I know where you sleep." Elspeth glared at her banshee granddaughter.

"We live in the same house. I know where you sleep too." Holly snickered and looked at her cousins for sarcasm support, but both women whistled and looked away. "Seriously? Where's the family support?"

Lila pointed at a sneering Elspeth. "You take the wicked witch on, you do it by yourself. Mock at your own risk."

Smiling sweetly at Holly, Elspeth dropped into the spare seat at the table. "We'll discuss your sass at another time, like at two am when you need your beauty sleep." Elspeth put a hand up and whispered to the table, "She really needs that beauty sleep."

"Hey," Holly protested, but settled down when Lila shook her head.

Lila rested her chin in her hands and stared at her grandmother. "Haven't seen you around meddling lately. You do know another body turned up?"

Elspeth's eyes darted around the bakery, cataloguing who sat where and who was within earshot of the Harrow table. "I've been busy. Figured you girls had all the help you need to solve the murder."

Elspeth refusing the chance to meddle? Now Lila knew her grandmother had a scheme afoot. Changing tactics, Lila frowned and leaned forward, pretending to scan Elspeth's face. "Are you trying a youth cream? For some reason, your skin looks lovely, almost like you're a teenager again." Lila sat back and waited for the fireworks.

Elspeth flinched and then growled. Shadows pooled around her chair. "How did you know, you meddling baker?"

"Know?"

"What?"

Xandie and Holly's questions collided with each other.

"I don't know if I should reveal all my tricks. I might need them to take your scheme down next time."

"Shoot," Elspeth growled and clutched the edge of the table. Shadows grew until a tiny dark storm cloud hung over the table. Intermittent bursts of lightning lit the cloud. A stampede of bodies rushed past the table as the bakery emptied of customers. Hester carried on cleaning up tables in the background, unconcerned. "I don't have schemes. I have magnificent plans that astound the residents of Point Muse."

"And frustrate the local law enforcement?"

"No need to swear and used that L word, Lila Marie Harrow." Elspeth pointed a finger at Xandie's sugar-comatose boyfriend. "Besides, I have a get out of jail free card that I can play when needed."

All the Harrow women stared at the police chief bear shifter. Who continued to munch on a honeybun, eyes glazed over, seeing nothing but the bun as he raised it to his mouth.

Xandie shrugged. "He can't help it. His whole family shuts down after too many honey buns, it's hilarious." She snickered and snapped fingers in front of Zach's face with no reaction. "See? Carry on fighting and ignore him." Xandie settled back into her chair with a smirk.

"I repeat, baker girl. How did you know?"

"Wasn't hard. Perky cheerleader? Always seems to pop up with a flatulent-cursed kitten in the center of erupting mayhem? Definitely an Elspeth trait."

"Hades' hairy..." Shadows forming a dark cloud over the table dissipated and Elspeth tapped her fingers on the tabletop. "I have to work on that."

Holly gaped at her grandmother. "You disguised yourself as a blonde cheerleader?"

Xandie chortled, holding her stomach. "Oh, that's classic. You've been prancing around us for the last few days and we had no clue." Xandie laid her head on the table, body shaking with rolling laughter. The snorting cut off abruptly as she jerked her head up. "Hang on, perky teenager? You gave me that cookie that made me squawk like a duck. You fiend." Xandie shook a fist at her grandmother.

"Never take a cookie from a stranger."

"You're not a stranger, we're related."

Elspeth cackled. "But you didn't know that then. You young things are so gullible."

Lila raised a hand, smirking. "Don't include me in that group. I've never taken sweets from a stranger and squawked like a duck."

"I guess I'll have to try something else to fool you. Won't I?" Elspeth grinned, blinding white teeth on show.

Lila shuddered. Elspeth plotting was enough to make an angel run away screaming. Speaking of Elspeth and her flatulent sidekick... "Where's Colin?"

Elspeth cleared her throat. "About Colin. I may have made a slight miscalculation in my potion ingredients."

Nash whimpered under the table as the kitchen door slammed open and another animal strutted out. The table shook as Nash leapt to his feet, howling.

Xandie and Holly hid their faces in horror.

"What did you do now, Elspeth?" Lila pointed a

trembling finger at the animal as it strolled up to the table.

Nash pressed himself against Lila, shuddering. "Bad." His low growl filled the room.

"Everyone's a critic." The former party known as Colin paused for a moment to pose. "I like it. Maybe felines aren't so bad."

Lila fake gagged. "That is not a feline. That's a Frankenstein creation." Half pug-half cat. Poor Colin, he was an unholy mismatch with a pudgy pug behind and a fuzzy orange feline face. Elspeth had outdone herself in crimes against mother nature this time.

"What in all Hades is that?" Matthew Grim, Point Muse's personal reaper, stood framed in the stairway to the upstairs apartment, horror creating a frozen mask upon his face.

"That is Elspeth and her quest to create havoc and mayhem." Lila rolled her eyes.

"Plus, she's been banned from anything to do with the Academy Founding Day celebrations. Elspeth couldn't help herself. She had to meddle," Holly muttered.

Matthew took a wide berth around Colin, coming to a halt next to Xandie's boyfriend. He shot a quick glance at his friend. "Is he okay?"

Xandie shifted the empty plate away from the bear shifter. "Honey buns. The Brauns curse to bear."

The three cousins dissolved into giggles.

Grim shook his head. "You Harrows are a menace. Don't you have a murder to investigate and a bake sale to judge?"

"Don't remind me," Lila grouched. "I might be a baker, but I'm not qualified to judge best stall. Some of those women take competition beyond a joke. It's cutthroat. Besides, I still need to find Rufus and have a chat"

Elspeth slapped the table. "You need to focus on that witch-banning P.T.A. I don't trust them. That's why I'm in disguise. As for Rufus, he'll be lurking around, don't forget he's a judge too. There's murder afoot and I can smell it."

"Ah, that might be me." Colin shivered and sagged. "Cats eat tuna. I'm a cat. Well, at least my head is."

"Hecate's inflamed digestion." Lila slapped a hand over her mouth and launched herself out of the chair. Beating a path to the bakery door, Lila shoved Holly to the side in her race for fresh air.

Dealing with the Harrow family should come with danger pay, or a gas mask.

Lila thumped on the locked door to the Alchemy shop that Rufus shared with Bertie Boxwood. "Open up, Rufus. We need to talk. I know you're in there. You have nowhere else to be until the bake sale judging tomorrow." The shop had the shades down, but through the cracks Lila could see a black figure pacing. "Best you answer my questions now or I'll send Elspeth over for another visit."

The figure paused and drifted closer to the door. "I can't talk right now," Rufus whispered.

Hecate save her from drama queens. "Rufus. Just let me in. We have to talk."

"Go away, Lila Harrow. I have a plan now. I've worked it all out. I'll talk to you after the bake sale judging." Rufus's voice receded and the lights flickered off.

"Argh," Lila hissed. "I will track you down, Rufus, you snake." Lila slapped the wooden shop door and stomped off. Old-fashioned lamp posts illuminated Main Street, giving it a nice old-world glow. Normally, late-night strolls in Point Muse were perfectly safe, but with a murderer on the loose... Lila shivered. At least her apartment lay only a few hundred meters away. Lila glanced up and down the road, her Harrow sense of impending doom pinging. A strange rustling noise sounded off to the side of the partially illuminated Main Street.

"Hello?" Lila peered down the street, but the town's charming streetlights couldn't exactly blast the shadows away. A noise, like the dry scrap of sandpaper, sounded again, this time closer.

"If that's you, Elspeth, revenge is sweet."

A hoarse chuckle sounded right next to her. Lila spun around and raised her fists just in case it wasn't Elspeth tormenting her.

A slow hiss built to a shriek, accompanied by a frantic dry raspy noise, like snake scales rubbing. Lila gritted her teeth and shuffled back until she stood under a lamp post, its limited light ringing her. A swaying shadow stood to the side, partially hidden by the shop, and just beyond the lamp post's meagre light.

"Stalking is a crime, not to mention cowardly. How about you step out and we talk face-to-face?"

The shadow failed to answer, but its swaying doubled in pace. Tiny little shadows slithered off from the figure's feet and headed toward Lila. The hissing increased as the shadows formed into small yellow and green snakes. Lila jumped onto the base of the lamp post. "What is it with snakes? Seriously? The town needs a snake catcher."

The shadow ceased swaying. "*Stay away*," the figure rasped, voice husky and rough.

"Stay away from who or what?" Lila hollered back. "I'm stuck on a lamp post. That's about as far as away as I can get from you currently." Lila squealed as tiny snakes coiled around the base of the lamp post.

"*Stay away.*"

"OMG, you already said that," Lila screeched. "More information is needed if you want me to stay away." She grabbed the lamp post tight. Right about now would be a great time for one manly reaper to swoop in to save the day and the snake-threatened damsel.

A low growl sounded from behind the shadow and twin red eyes flamed in the darkness.

Then again, a possessive hellhound racing to her rescue might be just as good as a sexy reaper. "Get her, Nash."

The twin red eyes surged forward, forming into a larger than average hellhound puppy. Nash snorted a red flame that flickered at the shadow.

Screeching, the figure retreated, its little snake minions withdrawing.

Nash howled a challenge and then galloped over to Lila, butting his head against her legs. "Pet safe," he huffed.

Lila rolled her eyes and slid down to the ground.

"How many times do I have to tell you? You're the pet, not me. *You.*"

Nash smirked, tongue out.

"I'll admit I'm grateful for the rescue, but that still doesn't mean I'm your pet." Lila smothered Nash's nose in kisses. "But you've definitely earned big cuddles."

The puppy had arrived just in time to chase her shadow stalker off after it delivered its ambiguous message. What was clear was that someone didn't like her investigating Britney Cygnus' murder.

"Tough cookies." Lila Harrow was a baker witch on a mission and no shadowy villain would get in her way...

EIGHT

"Against my better judgement, my fellow Muses have decided to allow you access to the bake sale." Clio, the green-haired muse, eyed Elspeth doubtfully. "They're swayed by the Harrow connection to the Great Library of Alexandria."

The implication? The grumpy muse didn't give a sugar drop about Elspeth's connections. Lila forced a smile. "I can't blame you, Clio. But Elspeth has always dedicated herself to the betterment of the Academy." And if Clio believed that Lila could probably sell her a vacation home in Tartarus.

"My dear Clio, all I have ever wanted to do was to help the Academy. The educational heart of Point Muse." Elspeth adjusted Colin on her hip. "Even my little baby, Colin, is here to support the

Academy." She pointed to the jaunty little hat, in the school colors of aqua and silver, tied to Colin's head.

At least Elspeth had managed to change her crime against nature into a full-bodied pug again instead of the half feline monstrosity she'd seen yesterday.

"Only a manly pug like myself could carry off a hat in these colors." Colin eyed the muse up and down. "Love the green on you, toots. Ever considered a canine companion?"

Clio shuddered. "Just don't mess up. Next time I won't be so easy to sway." The muse sniffed. "This is the Founders' Day celebration week and should be celebrated with pomp and ceremony and instead it's been traumatic and disruptive."

Lila nudged Elspeth out of the way and stood next to Clio. "It's quite tragic what happened to poor Britney."

"She had a strong connection to the school. We cared about her input." Clio paused before delicately adding, "The drama that sometimes accompanied her gestures, on the other hand, could be very disconcerting. Of course, I'm not one to speak ill of the dead," she hurried to add.

Lila ignored Elspeth's snort behind her. "Britney

dedicated herself to the school, but she did have an abrasive personality."

"Britney had a talent for raising substantial financial support for the Academy, but since her children are no longer at the school, the rules required that she step down from her position within the P.T.A. Although her continued support for the Academy was, of course, encouraged."

"But Britney didn't want to release her hold over the P.T.A., I take it?"

Clio nibbled at her lip. "Ms. Cygnus refused to relinquish her power. By rights, the position should have gone to the next in line."

Possible suspect? "Who might that be?"

"Chloe Sylvis. Obviously, her daughter still attends, and both are extremely active within the school environment."

And coincidentally, the lifelong mortal enemy of the swan shifter. "Anyone else who may have clashed with Britney or Chloe?"

The muse glanced over her shoulder at the crowded hall. "Although no longer an active member of the P.T.A., Emmaline Winchester has always been extremely generous in her support of our school."

"But..."

"Lately, Ms. Cygnus had to chase said support.

I'm afraid there's been a few fiery exchanges. Ms. Winchester is quite set in her ways. The situation has improved since the younger Ms. Winchester arrived in town for a visit, though." Clio cleared her throat and smoothed her flowing Grecian gown. "Excuse me, but the bake sale needs my organized touch." She gave the lurking Elspeth a gimlet stare. "Best behavior, Harrow."

"Always," beamed Elspeth. She waited for the woman to disappear into the crowd. "What an iron pants. Muses used to be fun to hang with. Their kids are sulky demigods."

"Shush. You want to get thrown out again?"

Elspeth snorted. "They could try."

Lila grunted. "They already did. You had to sneak back in as a glamoured teenager. Remember?"

"Talk to the hand, Lila Harrow." Elspeth shoved a wrinkled hand into her granddaughter's face before blending into the crowd.

"We'll all regret that decision, sooner rather than later," Matthew Grim whispered in Lila's ear.

His breath tickled the sensitive spot while electric chills zapped along the side of her neck. Dratted reaper, sneaking up on her. Lila spun, her face close to Matthew's as he leaned over.

Both froze, their mouths a scant distance away from each other.

"That's so sweet. But it's action stations right now. Mushy stuff later." Aunt Winifred bustled between the couple and grabbed Lila. "I need help setting up the bake sale table."

Lila cleared her throat and dragged her gaze away from the too tempting reaper. "I'm a judge. Isn't that a conflict of interest?"

Winifred snorted. "You're a Harrow first. Now chop, chop, minion. I have boxes in a pile near the hall exit."

Matthew jerked back, his face pale. "I have to circulate. Make sure Elspeth hasn't caused any Harrow related mayhem." He spun on the spot and marched off in the opposite direction to Lila.

"I'm quite impressed, Lila dear. The reel-him-in-and-let-him-go technique does seem to spark interest."

"I. Don't. Know. What. You're. Talking. About," Lila ground out and stomped away from the crowd hungering for baked goods. "Nosy family butting in." So what if the reaper sometimes short-circuited her brain functions with his hooked nose, gray eyes and floppy hair? Didn't mean kissy, kissy was automatically involved...yet.

Argh. Now she couldn't get that image out of her head, and she didn't even have the mouthy hellhound, Nash, to distract her. Her mom had snaffled her puppy first thing for a health checkup. Amelia Harrow took her role as a town veterinarian very seriously. "Where are those Hecate-cursed boxes of Winifred's?" Lila groused as she reached the exit.

Casting around, she spotted a pile of bright pink boxes with her aunt's name bedazzled on the side. "Bingo." She grabbed the two boxes and hoisted them into her arms. "Geez, Winifred. These feel like bricks, not cakes and cookies."

Lila carefully balanced the boxes and turned to head back to the bake sale. Then she spotted Mildred, Emmaline Winchester's dour housekeeper, scurrying along the corridor toward the hall.

Mildred rushed past Lila and into the hall with Edie trailing behind her.

The youngest Winchester drew to a halt when she reached Lila. "Another day, another fundraising torture."

"Try living here full-time and being the stall judge. No matter which competitor I pick, everyone else will hate me, including my own family." Lila juggled boxes. "Plus, waiting for Elspeth to lower the chaos boom is tiring. She's planning something. I can feel it in my baker bones."

"If it gets us out of the bake sale, I'm all for your grandmother creating mayhem."

"You say that now, but you haven't seen the fallout yet." Lila shouldered her way into the hall full of tables and overflowing baked goods. Bright colors, balloons and high sugar content seem to be the theme this year. "Thank Hecate's sweet tooth I left Nash with my mother. This amount of icing would send him into a sugar coma."

"I wish I could leave Emmaline at home." Edie grimaced. "She wants the bake sale to be perfect and is directing Mildred and me like an ironfisted dictator."

Lila wound through the crowd toward her aunt's stall. "I thought since she didn't have any kids at the Academy, she couldn't be a part of the P.T.A.?"

Edie snorted and pushed her glasses back up on her nose. "Because she's donated so much time and money to helping the school, they mostly just let her do what she wants. Or at least, they did."

"Until Britney."

"Until the swan put the brakes on Emmaline controlling the P.T.A.," Edie admitted. "My Great-Aunt wants the bake sale to be a huge success. She expects Chloe Sylvis to become the new head of the P.T.A. and Emmaline thinks Chloe will do the same as Britney and edge her out. She won't be impressed if that happens."

Lila shook her head. "Who knew the education world had so much intrigue?" Lila dumped the boxes down on Winifred's table.

"Careful, Lila. We don't want my rock cakes to be broken before judging." Winifred Harrow winked at her niece.

"Don't remind me." Puffing, Lila linked arms with Edie. "Let's stroll, so I can peruse the competitors' offerings."

"Who else is judging?"

"My cousin, Xandie, and Rufus Moon."

Edie grimaced. "He's kind of slimy, always seems to be lurking."

"Speaking of the lurkee, have you seen him today?"

"I saw him and Chloe Sylvis arguing this morning at the Academy's back entrance. Mildred almost ran them down. Emmaline was not impressed with the public display. *Or* with Mildred's driving."

"Rufus is relatively harmless. An idiot, but still harmless." And sneaky. She still had questions for the poison peddler, and she wasn't taking no for an answer.

"People are buying up a storm already. I think your bakery will run at a loss today." Xandie snuck up next to Lila. "Would anyone notice if we skipped out the back before judging?"

Lila pointed at the two colorful-haired muses stationed at each exit. "The neon hair fuzz has cut off all escape."

Xandie sighed. "Foiled again."

"Suck it up, buttercup. We just need to get today out of the way and all we have left as the Founder's Day luncheon and the fashion show. Then we're done for the year."

"Bring it on." Xandie rounded on Lila and lowered her voice, "What is this I hear about you being stalked up a lamp post last night?"

"What? Are you okay, Lila?" Edie Winchester bit her lip. "Point Muse isn't the safe, calm town I thought it was."

"We're the supernatural murder capital of the world. Calm? Point Muse is not." Lila ran her fingers through her long curly brown hair. "Some snake-loving, shadow-lurking freak sent a pack of snakes after me. I decided to take a closer look at the town's lamp post. That's all."

"Pit, nest, or den. Not pack."

"What?" Xandie and Lila stared at Edie.

She blushed. "Sorry. Freaky snake lover here. A bunch of snakes are called a pit, nest, or den. But getting the reptiles to work as a concerted group is not normal behavior at all."

Lila pursed her lips. "Know of anything or anyone who could control snakes? Like a Pied Piper?"

"That's rats, not snakes, Lila." Xandie elbowed her cousin.

"Whatever." Lila shrugged. "Any ideas?"

"The only supernatural I know that can control a nest of snakes would be a Lamia. Snakes love them. Will do whatever they are told."

"Makes sense when we know there's a Lamia poison supplier in town. What's a better way to get the venom than to milk it yourself?" Lila shuddered. "That sounds so wrong."

Edie nodded. "It would make sense. Was there anything strange about your shadow stalker?"

"It swayed and hissed? That's all I can give you. Whoever it was stayed in the shadows, told me to stay away. Oh, and when Nash turned up, it took off, so I guess it's terrified of hellhounds. Does that sound like a Lamia, Edie?"

"I have no clue, but it definitely sounds weird. I like snakes, but Lamias are beyond my expertise. We need to find someone who knows more about Lamias."

"Oh. Me. Me." Xandie waved her hand like a little girl. "I can use the Library to research Lamias."

Lila patted her overly enthusiastic cousin on the back. "The job is all yours, bookworm. We'll meet up after the bake sale at the Library."

"Mind if I come along? Lamias are interesting. My mother used to frighten me with stories about Lamias eating kids who wouldn't go to sleep. She was terrified of them."

Lila winked at Edie. "The more sleuthing minions the better."

"OMG. This is the last straw. The last straw. Do you hear me?" Chloe Sylvis' strident tones cleaved through the excited babble of the bake sale.

Lila turned and focused on the shifter.

The curvy, sandy haired woman stood next to her stall, pointing accusingly at an empty lockbox.

Hurrying over, Lila pulled up next to the cotton-candy pink stall. "What's wrong?"

"I've sold half of my stock already. I just popped over to the next stall for a moment. I come back and someone's stolen my money and rearranged my stock." She pointed at a small plate of bright orange pies. "My poor little persimmon pies have been pawed. This is a conspiracy. You're all out to get me."

And her family called Lila a drama llama? "I'm sure no one has it in for you, Chloe. It's just a mix-up. Maybe the Muses decided to collect your money already? Because you've sold so much compared to everyone else, I mean."

Modified, Chloe sniffed. "I still feel like I'm being targeted. Now I know how that swan felt at the top. It really *is* a lonely job." She flicked her hair over her shoulder. "Well, no matter what certain people think, I'm not going down without a fight. I was born to be the head of the P.T.A."

Life goals. "The Muses have already appointed you to the job?" Lila maneuvered Chloe off to the side so people could get to the stall. Marion, Chloe's daughter, ignored her mother's histrionics and kept on serving baked goods.

"Unofficially, of course. But continuity needs to be kept up. The Academy must always push on and I'm the best at achieving that. No matter what anyone else says."

"I bet you are," Lila muttered under a breath.

"Excuse me?" The bunny shifter glowered at Lila.

Pretending to cough, Lila patted her chest. "Just a frog in my throat. What people are against your appointment?"

"As I said, it's unofficial until the head mistresses announce it. But people are just jealous. Jealous wannabes holding on when they should have given up already." Chloe waved off Lila's comment.

"I heard somebody else was angry. You and Rufus were seen arguing."

"Let me guess. Emmaline Winchester? Talk about holding on like I said." Chloe rolled her eyes like her teenage daughter. "Rufus and I had a difference of opinion. That's all."

"Care to share the difference of opinion?"

"No." Chloe smirked at Lila. "If you want to know more, get your pet bear shifter to arrest me. Now if you don't mind, I have a stall and missing money to get back to." The woman flounced off to her stall.

"Bunny shifters are predators. Never turn your back on them." Elspeth shoveled half a pink-colored cupcake into her mouth. The other half she offered to Colin.

"What have you done to the poor dog?"

"All good, toots. It's the best way to travel and people keep feeding me. My dame should have thought of this earlier." Colin wiggled in the cloth baby carrier that Elspeth had draped over her nonexistent chest. Cupcake crumbs tumbled to the floor as he munched.

Lila gagged. Her emerald, neon green wig-wearing grandmother wore a matching-colored pantsuit which now sported a Colin appendage growing out of her stomach. How much worse could the bake sale get?

"He's been poisoned." Marion Sylvis' shriek filled the room and stilled the babbling, baked good-loving crowd.

Spinning toward the stall, Lila watched as Rufus Moon stiffened like a board and white froth bubbled out of his mouth. He jerked for a moment before dropping to the floor. Half a persimmon pie fell from his hand before he hit the deck.

Lila rushed to the body and felt for a pulse. She shook her head at Xandie. "Someone needs to get Braun here as soon as possible."

"No need." Xandie pointed as both her bear shifter police chief boyfriend and Point muse's own reaper rushed over.

"Let me guess. Poison?" Zach Braun, police chief, raised an eyebrow at Xandie before speaking quietly into a small black radio.

"The way that poor man stiffened after eating the cake and his collapse, I'd say it was a large amount of snake venom. Paralyzed his diaphragm immediately so he couldn't breathe." Edie gulped. "Poor man."

Everyone stared at Rufus, then Chloe Sylvis' cake stall and the pink plate with orange persimmon pies upon it.

She backed away, hands to mouth. "It wasn't me. I swear I didn't kill Rufus. You're all against me."

Elspeth nudged Lila. "See, it isn't only me that causes mayhem."

It seemed like someone was after Queen Elspeth's mayhem crown.

Hopefully that was the only thing they were after…

NINE

"At least we got out of judging best stall this morning. That's a silver lining, isn't it?" Lila offered the room a lopsided smile.

"Not for Rufus Moon," Elspeth cackled but all the lights refused to flicker. Lila's grandmother shot the Library ceiling a mutinous glare. "Fun police."

"The Library doesn't appreciate anyone playing games, except for her." Xandie winked at Elspeth.

"Buzzkill." Elspeth ignored both her grand-daughter and the library. She used her toe to poke her slumbering pug. "Shouldn't you be defending my honor?"

Colin opened one eye. "Against the library? You off your fruit loops, sweetheart?"

"The betrayal." Elspeth clasped her hands to her

bony chest and collapsed dramatically against the velvet couch.

Matthew Grim pointed to Lila, who sat opposite him. "See. That's who you get it from."

Lila bared her teeth. "Take that back, you vile insulter of my good name."

"Can't you leave the children at home?" Theo, Xandie's black cat guardian, strolled into the library, with his pet imp, Horatio, riding on his back.

Horatio, resplendent in a lilac jogging suit with his name bedazzled on the bottom, held out his arms to Nash.

The hellhound jumped up and bounded over to Theo.

Horatio gathered himself and leapt onto the puppy.

Theo hissed and turned his back, his fluffy tail hitting Nash in the face. "Traitor. I refused to acknowledge this obsession you have for each other."

Nash collapsed on the ground next to Lila and Horatio spread out on the hounds back, star-fishing, his arms and legs spread wide.

"Poor Theo." Lila patted her leather chair. "Want a snuggle?"

"I. Am. Not. A. Cat," Theo hissed, his whiskers trembling.

"Actually, you kind of are."

"When you least expect it, Lila Marie Harrow, I will strike. Revenge will be mine and it will be epic." Theo sniffed and strutted out of the library, tail stiff with outrage.

"Wow. He does offended really well." Poor Theo, the feline guardian to the Library, had actually started life as an ancient Greek teenager. Unfortunately, while Theo had guzzled mead from a hipflask and read scroll porn in the stacks of archived scrolls, a demon-possessed Julius Caesar had burnt the supernatural Great Library of Alexandria down to the ground. The only way the supernatural entity had been able to save the teenager was to change him into an immortal black cat guardian to the Library. And now, Xandie, as the Librarian, was stuck with the mouthy feline.

"Get over it." Xandie tapped the desk she perched on. "Library? Everything you have on Lamias and snake venom used in poisons, please."

Lila winked at the reaper as he braced himself. The Library had a habit of being eager to please, which generally lead to erratic flying literature and head wounds. Not one to disappoint, the Library's lights flickered overhead, and multiple scrolls rose into the air, dueling as they flew toward Xandie. A heavy, red velvet-embossed tome lifted ponderously into the air.

Matthew flinched as the heavy book moved slowly through the air before dropping onto the desk, right next to Xandie.

She snagged the scrolls out of the air. "It's all fun and games until someone gets an eye poked out." Xandie winked at the reaper. "We've never actually had a workplace-related accident here. I count that as a win."

"Enough chitchat. What do we have on Lamias?" Lila tapped her fingers on her leg. She needed to find a clue before Elspeth caused more mayhem or the body count rose.

Xandie flicked through the book and then reached for the scrolls, unwinding and quickly perusing them. "Soooo..." She drew the word out, clearly thinking her words through. "Says here an ageing Greek Queen did the deed with Zeus and had some kids by him."

Elspeth snorted. "Oh, I can see where this is going. Typical gods, can't keep it in their pants." She paused dramatically and pretended to swoon. "Oh, woe is me, Zeus and I bumped uglies, now his wicked wife is out to get me."

"Pretty much," Xandie agreed. "Hera wasn't

happy and forced his lover to kill her kids and cursed her with insomnia. To help her out, Zeus gifted her with shape shifting and the ability to remove her eyes to sleep. But his gifts gave her serpentine qualities."

"Serpentine? That's snake, right?" What did Lila know? Her expertise lay in copious amounts of sugar.

"Half snake, half woman. Supposedly." Matthew frowned. "Aren't Lamias rare though?"

"Only a few bloodlines carry the gene for a Lamia. But that information is buried so deep the Library has no record of it. At least for now. The Library's still looking."

"Don't bury the lead, book girl. How do we kill the reptile?" Elspeth thumped the arm of the chair. "I can't abide reptiles. All cold and slimy." She shuddered and gathered Colin up to her chest. "My Colin's so much better than a nasty snake."

Colin coughed and spluttered, his tongue hanging out. "Enough with the love, sweet cheeks. You'll send me to an early grave without lunch and dinner. And that's no way for a manly pug like myself to go."

Elspeth released Colin and placed him at her feet.

"Death and injury weakness, now." She snapped her fingers at Xandie.

"Right." Xandie scanned one of the oldest scrolls for more information.

Edie held a hand up. "I don't have a lot of knowledge about Lamias, but I do know they can control other snakes and my mother once told me a fairytale about a Lamia being able to change from human to snake woman like a shifter. That means the Lamia here in Point Muse could be anyone."

"She's right. It could be the person standing right next to you for all we know." Lila sucked on her lip. How did one track down a mythical shadow-lurking, cold-blooded shifter? "Do the scrolls say anything else?"

Xandie nodded. "It mentions rosemary and salt sprinkled on a Lamia will disable it momentarily and fire can finish it off. Likewise, a blessed silver knife can kill it. Apparently, they carry a terrible stench of decay and bodily functions around them."

"Plus, normal snakes don't like cinnamon, lime and garlic and if the Lamia is part supernatural reptile, she might hate them too." Lila patted herself on the shoulder for a job well done. She glared as everyone stared at her, including one attractive and annoying reaper. "What? I read. I'm not just about recipes, you know."

Matthew cleared his throat. "It's more the

congratulatory pat on your shoulder. That freaked us out."

"Hey, if you can't tell yourself job well done, who will?" Lila glared around the room.

"Loser," Elspeth coughed the word into a hand before beaming at her granddaughter. "Keep telling yourself that, sweetie. You do you." She turned back to the others and fake gagged.

"I can see you, Elspeth. The next time you need a sugar hit, you're banned. I give you nothing. Nothing, do you hear me?" Lila raised her voice.

Xandie leaned over and whispered to the reaper and Edie, "It's a family thing. Lila inherited the drama gene from Elspeth. When it comes down to it, it's all our grandmother's fault."

"And now my favorite betrays me." Elspeth mimed a dagger to the chest and then pointed an electric, blue-painted nail at the Librarian. Electricity arced around the tip. "If you weren't immune to magic because of the Library, I'd zap you for that nasty slur."

Forestalling the family squabbles, Nash jumped to his feet, whining. Horatio, the imp hung off the hellhound's ear by one hand, cheering wildly.

The door slammed open and Holly, Lila's third

cousin, stood framed in the door, her short bobbed brown hair in wild disarray.

Lila groaned and dropped her head into a hand. "Let me guess. We have another body?"

Holly looked confused for a moment. "No, I'm just running late for work. But I wanted to tell you, if you need to talk to Bertie Boxwood, the alchemist, you have to go now. He's packing up the shop and vacating Point Muse."

"Well, well. Little Bertie Boxwood doing a fly-by-night. What a surprise." Elspeth sniffed. "I told him when he took on Rufus, that man's dodgy dealings would bring him down." She rubbed her hands. "I'm wondering if he's having a going out of business sale?"

"Stand down from potential sales, old woman. We've got two murders to solve." Lila jumped up and clapped her hands. "Let's do this." She pointed at Xandie. "You're still on research detail. We need the bloodlines of a Lamia. See who we've got hiding in Point Muse." Lila swiveled and pointed at the reaper. "You need to shadow Braun. See what he knows."

"I'll check and see if my bosses know anything, they deal with a lot of different deaths. There might be other similar reports."

"Since Holly works at the Elysian Fields Funeral Home and her bosses are twin necromancers related to the Greek ferry man, Charon, it's good bet they might know something. Lurk and see what you can find." Lila clapped her hands.

"I suppose I'll just wander around, nose to the ground. Who knows what I might be able to sniff out?" Elspeth winked.

"As long as you don't kill anyone or get arrested, go for it." Lila strode toward the Library door and her cousin. "Time's a wasting, Banshee. We've got murders to solve, and you can drop me down to Bertie's shop."

Nash shook off Horatio and bounded after Lila.

"I told you. I know nothing. He just rented a portion of my shop, that's all." Bertie Boxwood stroked his moustache with a shaking hand.

She'd be anxious too if she had to get around town with that monstrosity of facial hair. Last time Lila had run across Bertie, he'd sported a Dumbledore-like beard. Unfortunately, he now showcased a drooping gray handlebar moustache, the ends of which tickled his chin. Lila shuddered. The idea of facial hair tasting her food first freaked her out. Forcing her mind away from rabid facial hair, she focused on the fleeing alchemist. "Give it up, Bertie. We all know you dabble on the dark side when you need to. Besides, you play poker with Elspeth, you must have a dark side."

Bertie straightened. "Correction. I lose to Elspeth, and I've never played with poison. I just may have the occasional shady transaction. But that's all." Bertie grabbed a plain black, zip-up bag and shoved a pile of leather-bound books inside.

"So why are you running?" Lila walked around the shop, trailing fingers over the shelves. The atmosphere had certainly changed within the store. Paperwork lay scattered on the desk and floor and empty potion bottles lay on their sides.

Nash sniffed an empty bottle and then coughed and spluttered, swiping at his nose.

Lila bent down to wipe the hound's muzzle. "Seriously? You're as curious as a cat or Colin on a snack hunt." Standing, Lila gazed at the anxious alchemist. "What's going on, Boxwood? Details now or my next visit I'll have Elspeth in tow."

"As a threat, that's surprisingly effective." Bertie smoothed his moustache. "I warned Rufus that dabbling in poison in Point Muse wasn't a good idea.

Too many loose cannons with an axe to grind, but he wouldn't listen. But I couldn't..." The alchemist trailed off.

"He paid you in cash up front. You couldn't say no."

Bertie nodded, shamefaced, at Lila. "I had some debts that needed settling. I couldn't see the harm, but I did warn him about some issues in town. Told him to stay away, but he didn't listen."

"The Cygnus and Sylvis feud."

"Correct. Never get between two warring clans, and certainly don't provide the same poison to both sides."

"What happened?"

"He got greedy, thought he could cut out the Lamia supplier and somehow produce the poison through his own connection, then sell at an increased price to the clans."

"The Lamia supplier wasn't impressed."

"Rufus swore that something was following him. He kept finding those horrible little yellow and green snakes everywhere. Even in his bed." Bertie shuddered. "He decided to call a ceasefire and go back to the original supplier, but he only had a third-party contact, and they refused to take his calls. He was frantic, so he went to Brittany Cygnus."

The swan shifter? "Why go to a client he was planning to fleece extra cash from?"

"He thought she might know the supplier. The rumor is that their family once had a connection to a Lamia. He hoped she would get the supplier off his back."

Lila snickered. "From what I see, the swan shifter wasn't known for her mercy and compassion."

"She blackmailed him. Told him he had to drop the Sylvis as customers and give her ten percent of his profits and then she'd give him the name of the Lamia."

Lila jerked. Britney had known not just the supplier, but the actual Lamia as well. *Or were they one and the same?*

"Rufus caved in, didn't he?"

Bertie nodded. "Snakes freaked him out. I think Cygnus gave him the name the day she died. I saw them arguing. I don't think Rufus believed her, but then she turned up dead."

"The Lamia found out Brittany and Rufus knew its human name."

"I think so." Bertie swallowed convulsively. "I told him to just cut his losses and get out of town, but he decided to try one last score. I had no clue what he was doing, but I heard him talking about extra money coming in. I figured he might sell the Lamia's name for one last score before he left town."

Lila rolled her eyes. Either he tried to sell the Lamia's information or blackmailed the Lamia. Either way, he was a dead man... Literally. "That doesn't explain why you're running?"

Lifting his bag onto a shoulder, Bertie scuttled toward the back door of the Alchemy shop. "I don't want either the Lamia or the bunny shifter to think I know anything. I'm getting out of town before they drop me off at Elysian Fields Funeral Home in a pine box. I'm thinking I might start a new business elsewhere. Point Muse is way too hot." Bertie gestured with a shaking hand. "Feel free to poke around, but watch your back, Harrow. This Lamia takes no prisoners."

Lila waved Bertie off. "Look after yourself. I have Elspeth and the hellhound and a father who is Hades' right-hand man. I'll be fine."

Bertie nodded. "Look for Rufus' ledger. He wrote in it religiously. If there's any clues they will be in there. Happy hunting, Harrow." Bertie slammed the door behind him with an ominous bang.

"A mysterious ledger is a perfect clue." Lila rubbed a hand over her face. "Let's get sleuthing,

Nash. Before the law enforcement of Point Muse rumble to the fact Boxwood legged it and I'm searching his shop."

Nash pranced around the messy alchemy store, nose to the ground.

"Careful what you sniff, hound. Mom won't appreciate another doctor's visit so soon, remember?" Thankfully Hades had eased up on his second-in-command and had allowed her dad to settle back into Point Muse. Her mother was now occupied with nagging her father. Limited parental meddling was a blessing Lila couldn't refuse, but it meant that the veterinarian empath, Amelia Harrow, wasn't always available for hellhound injuries and babysitting now.

"If I were a dodgy poison ledger, where would I hide?" Lila wandered around, prowling through the room. She could disregard any hiding place out in the open. Sneaky poison peddlers would want incriminating evidence hidden where they could reach it quickly in case of a police raid. She peered around the room and focused on Rufus' office.

Lila opened the curtains closing the alcove office off from the rest of the Alchemy shop. "Just as much of a mess as the store." Lila poked through the papers on the floor and on the top of the desk. She opened drawers and cupboards. Unfortunately, nothing but empty vials met her searching. "Drat you, Rufus. Surely you have a safe somewhere hidden?"

Nothing stood out, except for the poison seller's heavy wooden desk. She ran a finger over the carved wooden frame that decorated the tabletop. Not the kind of furniture she expected Rufus to have, too expensive for him. *Good question.* How could a poison peddler who dabbled in blackmail afford an ornately carved antique desk?

"Unless it served another purpose like a hiding place." Lila sat down in front of the desk and slid her fingers over the wooden frame, pressing various spots until she heard a click and a secret wooden drawer slid out. "Eureka. Sneaky, sneaky Rufus." Lila pulled the drawer open. "Not big enough for cash, so there must be another drawer."

She slid a hand into the small drawer and came up with a vial of clear liquid that had an iridescent shine to it. The label printed on the outside indicated it belonged to the Cygnus/Sylvis clans.

"I think we have Lamia venom. Probably the last vial left before he sorted out his supply issue." Or until his supply issue sorted him out...permanently. She reached into the drawer again but only came up with a few invoices made out to the Cygnus and

Sylvis families for Lamia venom. "Not exactly a surprise."

Lila slid the file and the receipts into her jeans pocket and ran her hands over the desk again. Surely, if there was one secret drawer, there was another?

This time, one of the legs made to look like a decorative wooden column clicked and tilted forward. "Your sneakiness is nothing compared to Harrow nosiness, Rufus," Lila crowed and tilted the drawer forward until a small wad of cash and a skinny blue ledger fell out. "Harrow for the win."

Ignoring the cash, Lila flicked through the ledger. Rufus had been more organized than she expected. Poison names, dates bought, purchasers and normal snake venom suppliers were laid out, although some of the purchaser's names were just initials. Braun would have a field day if Lila let him have access.

Nash whimpered from just outside the small alcove.

"Just a minute longer, then I swear we'll get out of here and grab you an afternoon snack. Promise."

Lila flicked through the last entries. Both Britney and Chloe had purchased Lamia venom a few days before Britney's death. The very last transaction was a sale to Rufus from E. Winchester, dated the day

Rufus died. And the only E. Winchester who loved snakes was the youngest Winchester, Edie.

"What have you done, Edie?"

Nash let out of sharp yip of warning.

"Okay, okay. Hold your flames, hellhound."

Lila closed the ledger and stood. She moved to soothe Nash with one hand, the ledger held tight in the other. "Let's slide out the back door. We need to speak to Edie as soon as possible."

Shuffling to the door, Lila kicked papers out of the way as she opened it. "What a dump, Nash. No wonder Bertie bailed." She let her puppy out then made sure the door latched behind her. Couldn't be too careful in Point Muse.

Nash's rumble of warning was the only tip-off Lila received before something sprayed both her and Nash in the eyes.

Lila dropped to her knees, the ledger forgotten on the ground beside her as she scrubbed at her eyes.

Nash mimicked her actions, but both their movements dwindled to sluggish quickly.

Lila slumped on the ground on her side. Her eyesight wavered and blurred as she descended into murky darkness.

A swaying noise accompanied by a dry rustle

sounded from in front of her, but all she could focus on was a shadowy blur with strange black goggles.

She squinted. Not goggles. Black-rimmed glasses just like the ones Edie wore. "Edie..." Lila slurred the youngest Winchester's name, but gave up when her tongue refused to work. The entity in front of her tore the ledger out from under Lila, accidentally tearing papers out at the same time.

The figure gathered up the loose papers and straightened, swaying for a moment before tucking Rufus' ledger away. Then the shadowy figure receded as darkness descended fully on Lila.

Grim and Braun would have a field day when they found her and Nash.

That's if they found them in time...

TEN

An incessant high-pitched beep battered at Lila's bruised brain. She tried to open one eye, but it remained stubbornly welded shut. "If this is Elspeth revenge, I swear I didn't touch her Witchshine stash, that was all Holly."

"Hey, you rat fink. We pinky swore we'd never reveal that," Holly griped from somewhere next to Lila.

"Holly? Why won't my eyes open? Did you glue them shut or has Elspeth claimed them as a sacrifice to a dark God?"

"I'm glad my granddaughter has an impressive grasp of my reputation, but no. This was all drama llama Lila."

"Hang on, Lila."

Matthew's rough voice sounded just above her, and his minty breath warmed her face. He gently pried up the corner of the bandages and eased them off. "The doctor told us we could take the eye pads off once you were conscious. Slowly open your eyes, give yourself time to focus." Matthew drew back but hovered close.

Lila grimaced and slowly opened her eyes. The room wavered for a moment before resolving into a sterile hospital room. "Aww, man. Hospital? How long have I been here for?"

"Just overnight. They needed to monitor the hellfire." Holly wiped a tear away. "We were very worried. Naughty, Lila."

"Not really my fault." Lila picked at the hospital bed. "You know how much I hate this place. No offence." She waved a hand in apology to any lurking medical practitioners.

"You're a Harrow." A doctor in a long white coat with colorful rainbow hair shrugged. "We'd rather not see you here either." She shone a small flashlight into Lila's eyes. "She's good to go. The hellfire worked a treat. She'll have sore eyes for a while but the redness on the skin surrounding the eyes will fade quickly. But thanks to her hellhound, she'll keep her sight intact. She's a lucky little Harrow. No evidence of cortical blindness, so once the papers are ready, she can discharge at the front desk. Try not to end up here again on my shift. I have a low tolerance for Harrow mayhem." The doctor disappeared out the door without another word.

"She's always held a grudge against your mother ever since Amelia edged her out of class valedictorian. Now she hates all Harrows and has access to debilitating medicines. Fun times." Elspeth winked at Lila.

"Someone sane please explain what happened?"

Holly held a hand up like a teenager and bobbed up and down. "Me. Me. I can tell."

Lila rolled her eyes and winced. "Ouch. Fine, just get on with it."

Holly perched on the side of Lila's hospital bed. "Apparently, while you were searching Bertie Boxwood's Alchemy shop, some nefarious assailant surprised you with a blast of King Cobra snake venom directly in your and Nash's eyes."

"So why aren't I blinded and where's my puppy?" Lila wailed and clasped hands over eyes. "Hecate's blind eyeballs. That hurts."

Holly patted Lila's knee. "Lesson to be learned? Shelve the drama llama. Your puppy is fine and being spoiled by my mom at Harrow House."

Lila sagged against the hospital-grade, non-fluffy pillow in relief. Aunt Winifred took spoiling to Olympic levels. Nash would be fine. "How did I end up in here?"

"Let me finish." Holly glared at her bedridden cousin. "Anyhoo…Nash knew it was snake venom and used hellfire to burn it out of both of you. He managed to crawl onto Main Street which is where Matthew found him. He got the two of you to the hospital and the healer. But Nash had pretty much cleared the venom out of both of you. Matthew notified the rest of us and mom grabbed your puppy for pampering after your mother gave him the all-clear. Now you're up to date, why were you attacked in the first place?"

Lila shot a chagrined look at her family and friends. "I spoke to Bertie before he bolted. Apparently, Rufus planned on cutting the Lamia supplier out. He wanted to source his own Lamia venom. I don't think the supplier was too impressed. Plus, Bertie thought Rufus might have tried one last score and sold the Lamia's name. I think the Lamia and the supplier are the same person, and they objected to the blackmail… *Violently.*"

"How did you get from interviewing Bertie to being blinded by snake venom?" Matthew leaned against a wall, his forehead furrowed as he glared at Lila.

"Bertie ran off but gave me permission to search the shop." Lila poked a tongue out at the disapproving reaper. "See? Not illegal. I found a couple of secret drawers in Rufus' desk."

Holly clapped her hands. "Awesome. What did you find?"

"A vial of some clear liquid with both swan and bunny shifter's names on the label, receipts with their names and..." Lila paused for dramatic suspense. "I found Rufus' ledger." She deflated. "That's when I headed outside, and the snake assassin spat venom at me. She literally ripped the ledger out from underneath me."

"But we all know snoopy Lila Harrow had already flicked through it. What did you see, Baker girl?" Elspeth tapped a brightly painted nail on the windowsill of Lila's hospital room. She stared outside and hummed for a moment. "Tell me you got something from my DNA instead of your grandfather's do-gooder genes."

"Yeah, I got your snooping ones." Lila rubbed a hand through her tangled curly brown hair. "Both Britney and Chloe bought venom just before the Swan died. But the day Rufus died, someone sold venom to him. The ledger didn't list whether or not it was Lamia venom."

"You said '*she literally ripped the ledger from you.*' Who is *she*? Why do I get the feeling you're avoiding telling us who it was?" Matthew arched an eyebrow. "Enough tiptoeing around the subject. Tell us."

"It's wrong. I know she didn't hurt anyone," Lila protested. She gripped the hospital blanket tight as she tried to make sense of it all.

Surely, she wouldn't hurt anyone. She wasn't like that. And if that were the case, someone had set out to frame her. But who hated the youngest Winchester enough to do that?

"Spit it out, granddaughter. Before I wither away."

"Parts of her have already withered," Holly muttered, diffusing Lila's anxiety.

"The notation in the ledger was *E. Winchester.*"

The room exploded.

Holly shook her head. "No way. Edie wouldn't hurt a fly."

Elspeth spun from gazing out the window. "*Winchester.* That family's bad news all around."

"We need Braun in on this. He can bring Edie

Winchester in for questioning immediately." Grim strode for the door.

"Stop," Lila raised her voice and winced as the noises echoed in her head. She gently rubbed her forehead. "I don't think it was her. I think she's being framed by the Lamia."

Elspeth blew a raspberry at Lila. "See? This is a problem with your grandfather's genetic make-up. Naïve do-gooder genes smother my cynical sneaki-ness and love of mayhem."

"Listen. It's too obvious. *E. Winchester* in the ledger, then suddenly a couple of murders happen, and the ledger appears with her name in it."

"She keeps snakes and her Great-Aunt has a connection to the Academy. She should at least be interviewed," Matthew pointed out logically.

"As long as she isn't railroaded into dual murder charges. Remember, she hasn't been in town very long. What kind of motive would Edie even have?"

"You'd be surprised what reasons people find for murder."

Elspeth marched to the door. "The Banshee can take you home to Harrow House and settle you in. I'm sure your reaper will play nicely with law enforcement while you're recuperating."

"And what will the wicked witch of Point Muse

do?" Elspeth's propensity for finding chaos and mayhem was world-famous. Elspeth let loose on the town after a grandchild had been attacked could be compared to giving a megalomaniac interested in world domination the keys to the country's nuclear armament.

Elspeth beamed at the room. "I've decided to turn a few rocks over and see what slithers out. The best kind of fun. Tootles." Finger waving, the wicked witch of Point Muse disappeared out the door.

"Why do I have a bad feeling about letting Elspeth loose?"

"Because you're one of the few sane members of your family," Matthew pointed out.

"Hey," Holly protested the reaper's comment, then shrugged. "Really, he isn't far-off."

Matthew pointed his pen-sized scythe at Lila. "Try to stay away from trouble for a few hours while I liaise with Braun."

"I'm a baker, remember? Trouble finds me, not the other way around," Lila yelled at Matthew's retreating back.

"Welcome to the world of Harrow sleuthing." Holly grabbed a make-up bag and rummaged through until she found a giant-size brush. "Aha."

Lila eyed the torture implement warily. "What's that for?"

"What does it look like it's for? Time to tame the rat's nest that has settled in your hair. Hecate knows why that reaper didn't run out of the room screaming. Must be love."

Lila fought the red that flamed her cheeks. The Harrow women's preoccupation with a certain brooding reaper boarded on obsession. But if he hadn't run screaming away from her family already, then maybe he might stick around...

"This is worse than listening to the Academy talent show."

"Don't fight the pampering or it will bury you." Xandie crossed her arms over her chest. "Besides, you were interviewing a witness without backup. You deserve the hellish pampering."

"I had backup. I had Nash." Lila ran a hand over her slumbering hero. He really had come to her rescue. Between expending all his energy with using hellfire and Winifred's pampering, he was all tuckered out.

"First rule of the sleuthing club... Always take backup who can actually call for help."

"Technically, Nash can talk when he needs to," Lila replied.

"Don't spout logic to me, Lila Marie Harrow." Xandie bared her teeth. "No more hospital visits. Got it, Lila?"

"Why, when people tell me off, do they use my middle name?"

"More impact and guilt, dear. Harrows do guilt extremely well." Winifred bustled around the cozy sitting room in Harrow House and fluffed Lila's pillow as she reclined on the couch.

"I'm not an invalid, you know. They only kept me in overnight as a precaution." Truth be told, she couldn't believe her attack only happened yesterday. Felt like days ago.

"Well, you were lucky, and the Academy has nothing scheduled until tomorrow. So, it's rest time."

"Aren't I too sick for Academy functions? I'm just out of the hospital," Lila whined to her aunt.

"Suck it up and suffer through like the rest of us do, cousin." Xandie glared at Lila.

"Can't even have a pity party without Harrow naysayers turning up."

Winifred shoved a plate of chocolate chunk

cookies at her. "Eat so you aren't hangry anymore. You have visitors."

Harrow House creaked a warning as a knock sounded on the front door.

Generations of Harrow witches had lived, loved, and spelled within its walls. As such, the old Victorian had become sentient and as stubborn as any Harrow witch. It had a nasty habit of moving walls or stairs when it was upset...or mischievous. And as an early warning system, it rocked. Lila slid a foot to the floor and rubbed it forward and backward. "Thanks, house. You rock."

The walls creaked again, and its lights glowed brightly for a moment before the door to the sitting room flung open. Edie Winchester flew in, red hair streaming behind her and her black-rimmed glasses askew. "I swear, I didn't attack you, Lila. I'd never hurt anyone, and especially not with snake venom."

Lila sighed and leaned back on the couch. "The rumor mill is working overtime, I take it?"

Xandie shrugged. "Frankly, I'm surprised it's taken twenty-four hours to reach her. I thought the gossip queens were more on-point than that."

Edie collapsed to her knees next to the couch. "You have to believe me. I would never hurt you or Nash or murder anyone."

Lila patted Edie on the shoulder clumsily. She wasn't exactly known for her warmth and compassionate nature, but more for her sugar and sarcasm skills. "I know you didn't do it. Someone set you up. We just have to find out who."

Heaving a sigh of relief, Edie sat back on her heels. "It's around town that Bertie Boxwood named me as the killer before he ran."

"Rufus Moon was a poison peddler and kept a hidden ledger. Britney Cygnus and Chloe Sylvis both bought Lamia poison from him. Unfortunately, the day Rufus died, someone using the name E. Winchester supposedly sold him venom. I found a vial of liquid with Chloe and Brittany's names on it."

Edie stood and walked to an empty chair. "Why frame me? What have I done to anyone in Point Muse?"

Xandie answered the perplexed woman, "It might not even be about you. This could be just related to the Winchester name. Someone with a grudge against your family, maybe?"

"I get the impression from my parents that the Winchesters weren't exactly joiners in the community. They had a reputation for being reclusive. My grandmother married young and had little to no contact with the family after she left. She never really spoke about them either. She died last year, so I decided to look up my Great-Aunt and get to know her. My parents weren't fond of the idea, but it wasn't their choice. Now I can see why my grandmother wouldn't talk about her family or Point Muse." Edie sagged.

"Not what you expected?" Lila fought the urge to let Winifred pamper the youngest Winchester. Poor Edie had thought she'd be welcomed into the loving arms of her estranged family. Instead, she'd ended up with cranky Emmaline Winchester and the lurking Mildred.

"Not really. I don't think Great-Aunt Emmaline is interested in family. She won't talk about my grandmother, except to sneer, and she hates the town. As soon as I can, I'm heading back home. That's assuming I'm not arrested for multiple murders."

"Lila won't let that happen, dear." Winifred held the plate of cookies out. "Cookie? The sugar will help. And don't worry, Lila didn't bake them." Winifred winked to the room.

"No one likes my cookies." It was enough to give a baker a complex, but her aunt wasn't wrong. Her cookies tasted like sawdust no matter what recipe she used. Lila tapped her chin thoughtfully. "Are there any other Winchesters that could have sold venom to Rufus?"

"There's only myself, my parents, and Emmaline left. That's it. My parents are in an RV doing a tour around America. So, it isn't them. And Emmaline is in a wheelchair. Plus, she hates reptiles with a passion. There's no way she'd sell venom to Rufus. Looks like I'm the only logical suspect."

Elspeth charged into the room. Her iridescent mermaid-green-and-blue wig streamed behind her. "Stop the presses. I have a lead." She clapped her hands. "I've always wanted to say that."

"Move it or lose it, sweet cheeks. You can't stop the Colin train once it's started." Colin, Elspeth's talking pug, waddled behind her as fast as his pudgy paws could take him.

Lila eyed her way-too-excited grandmother. "Do I want to know or is ignorance bliss?"

"Not this time," Elspeth rushed her words out with a squeal. "We're going on a road trip," she crowed and punched her fists into the air.

Who knew an elderly woman could be so addicted to road trips?

ELEVEN

"Why? Why would you do that? It's just plain evil." Lila drew her bakery van to a shuddering stop with a screech of brakes. She wrenched the door open and launched herself out. She collapsed to the ground and sucked in deep shuddering breaths of fresh air.

"My Colin has a stomach issue. It's rude to bring attention to people's medical conditions." Elspeth hopped out of the van, Colin in her arms. "Honestly, I thought we'd raised you better than that."

"You gave him tuna before we got in the van for an hour-long drive. You know he can't handle tuna."

"But my baby loves his seafood." Elspeth nuzzled a panting Colin.

"Hey, sweet cheeks, dial the love down. Did you brush your dentures this morning?"

Lila snorted tiny chuckles as she pushed herself upright. "Yeah, Colin is a sweetheart. How about we focus on your lead? We don't have long before we need to be back in Point Muse."

Elspeth dumped Colin on the ground, then smoothed her iridescent mermaid wig. "Fine. Now watch your mouth with Deirdre. She isn't as sweet as I am. You catch more flies with sugar, not sour. Got me?"

"Isn't the saying you catch more flies with honey than vinegar?"

"Whatever." Elspeth rolled her eyes and twitched her wig into place.

"Why are we here again?"

"Deirdre worked for the Cygnus family for decades. She knows where the bodies are buried." Elspeth paused. "Actually, probably literally. She's always had a strong back and questionable morals."

"Sounds like your kind of crony."

"She's too mean for me and she's a stingy poker player." Elspeth pointed to a blue peeling front door on a ramshackle cottage. "Tally-ho, baker. The murderer waits for no one."

Sighing, Lila trudged to the door and knocked a few times. Hopefully, Elspeth's lead would help her track down the murderer. Because she had a horrible feeling the body count wasn't over yet.

The peeling door swung open to reveal a hunched over, decrepit old crone with bright blue eyes and elegantly coiffed lavender hair.

"What do you want, Elspeth Harrow? You don't hold any of my IOUs." The woman started to close the door.

Elspeth shoved her foot in the gap, pushed the door open and sauntered inside. "Need a favor, Deirdre."

The old woman cackled, the noise rivaling Elspeth at her wicked witch best. "Why would I help you? You're a burr on my barnacles."

"Because..." Elspeth drew the word out. "I'll owe you a favor. *Anything*." Elspeth winked. "Interested?"

"Fine. But I ain't serving you tea and nibbles. Get to your business, then go." The woman eased herself into a well-loved recliner.

Elspeth gestured Lila forward. "My granddaughter wants to ask you a few questions about the Cygnus family."

"Heard about the baker. Thought she was in hospital though?" The older woman pointed to Lila's still slightly red-tinged skin around her eyes.

"Reports of my injuries were exaggerated." Lila cleared her throat. Elspeth had been right, this woman definitely seemed mean. "I need to know about the Cygnus clan."

"What about them?" Deirdre tapped her fingers on the TV remote. "Spit it out, girl. I got a full TV watching schedule."

"Capable of murder?"

Elspeth's crony subsided into a phlegmy snicker. "Always about the bodies. Anyone's capable of murder. But the Cygnus clan has poison down to a fine art. You gotta admire them for that."

Lila grimaced. Deirdre's raspy accent sounded like she smoked a-pack-a-day for the last hundred years, and she looked like it too. But if she could give her information about the Cygnus family, Lila could deal with Elspeth crowing. "Do you know if they dealt in Lamia venom?"

Deirdre twitched. "I always told that know-it-all, Bettina, it would end up getting out of hand. The family's been dabbling for generations, but Bettina amped up production."

"How many people has the Cygnus clan poisoned? And how on earth did they get away with so many murders for so long?"

"Ha." Deirdre slapped her bony thighs. "It's not

about the finality of death. The Cygnus family has created a market out of poisons. They ship worldwide. Most of their compounds are used as bases for everything from medicinal uses, chemical engineering and of course, good old assassination."

In what strange world could one work the phrase *good old assassination* into the conversation? "Some of their businesses were legit, but what about their feud with the Sylvis clan? Would either side resort to murder?"

Sneering until her dentures popped out, Deirdre took a moment to shove them back in before replying. "Cygnus and Sylvis hate each other. Neither side would spit on the other to put them out if they were on fire. And yes, both would happily murder the other, if they thought they could get away with it."

What on earth would cause a disagreement that lasted generations? "What caused the blood feud?"

"Depends on who you talk to." Deirdre pointed at a twitching Colin, who sat quietly at Elspeth's feet. "Keep that animal away from me. I've heard the damage he can do with his bodily functions."

"Just be glad the hellhound isn't here as well. Those two together are a menace," Elspeth muttered then speared the other woman with a look. "Don't dance around the subject. Spill it, Deirdre. I know you've got more gossip and an axe to grind."

"They turned me off without a pension after years of service. Just because I couldn't traipse up and down the stairs anymore." Bettina slapped the armrest on her chair. "But my brain still works, and I've seen things." She winked at Lila.

"Things like what started the feud?"

"This Cygnus family picked the same lot of land as the Sylvis clan did when Point Muse settled. The council at the time awarded the Cygnus clan the land."

"That's all?" Lila shook her head. This was all about one kid wanting what the other kid had? How petty could people be?

"Yep. Oh, there's been other issues throughout the years, but that's the biggest."

"How about Britney's side business?" Elspeth prodded.

"Maybe if you let me get a word in edgewise, Harrow." Deirdre sniffed. "Mean girl Barbie liked to torment people for financial gain."

"Blackmail."

Deirdre nodded at Lila. "The juicier the better. She had enemies all right and I know she had something big on the boil. She called, looking to talk about the old days with me. She was fishing for something but wouldn't tell me what." Deirdre grimaced. "She probably thought I'd asked for a cut of her take, but she hung up before I could ask."

Something decrepit Deirdre had said over the phone to Britney had probably tipped the swan into blackmailing the wrong person...*the murderer.* "What did you talk about?"

"This and that." Deirdre waved a hand dismissively. "We talked about the feud, how it started. The clan's standing in town, alliances and such."

Elspeth groaned. "Where's the juicy in that? No one would pay blackmail for old gossip."

"Hey, I don't gossip. But I did tell little swan about an old rumor that had floated around town. Before my time, of course," Deirdre hastened to add. "The story was that a girl from another clan fell in love with a Cygnus boy. The couple eloped without the permission of either family. Few weeks after the wedding, the girl came back alone. The family took her back in, but they hid her from Point Muse society. She supposedly became a recluse."

"And her husband?" A historical murder mystery had her cousin Xandie's name all over it.

"Never saw him again. It was believed there was a fatal accident, the girl never spoke about it again.

The Cygnus clan raised a stink, but whoever the other clan was, they closed ranks and the story got buried."

"And that's what Britney wanted to know about?"

"She hung up straight after."

"Do you know the name of the other clan?"

Deirdre shook her lavender-helmeted hair. "Nope, no clue. But Britney sure seemed interested."

Maybe she had a blackmail plan in place and just needed Deirdre to confirm a few points. Lila stood. "Thanks for the help, Deirdre. I appreciate it."

Deirdre snorted and stood, hobbling to her front door. "Don't care for no appreciation. Harrow owes me a favor. That's the only reason I did it. Now get out. I want to watch Witch Island. I need to know if Lorenzo and Miranda hook up."

Deirdre waited until they cleared the doorstep, then slammed the door shut behind them.

"Well, she's a withered soul on the vine of old age," Lila remarked caustically.

Elspeth shrugged. "She's cranky. It happens when the family you've worked for all your life dumps you without even a small pension. She's a tad bitter. Me? I just get revenge." Elspeth grinned, her white teeth on show.

Lila shuddered. Way too much shark in that smile for her to feel comfortable. "We need to find out who the other family was. I think it's important." Something niggled at Lila, something both Harrows had forgotten...

The door to the cottage flew open and a high-pitched shriek busted out as the crone appeared in the door. "Curse you, Elspeth Harrow." Deirdre shook her fist at the Harrow women as Colin galloped outside as fast as his pug legs could carry him. The crone retched on the porch before she rushed back inside.

Colin panted as he sped to a stop near Elspeth. "Not my fault. I have a delicate constitution."

That's what they'd forgotten. A gassy pug...

"My kingdom. My kingdom for a gassy pug," Lila muttered to Xandie, seated at her side.

"Stop murdering Shakespeare. And you shouldn't wish Colin's radioactive flatulence on anyone. Let alone the alumni luncheon." Xandie elbowed Lila in her side. "Fake it until you make it. We're honored guests, remember?" Xandie smiled at the other table guests.

"*You're* an honored guest. I'm cannon fodder in case Elspeth shows." Lila smiled sweetly at the green-haired muse who sat opposite her. Right next to Xandie sat Edie, then Emmaline Winchester. Various other past Academy attendees were squeezed in around them. "How long do we have to suffer through this luncheon?" Lila whispered.

"Until the speeches are finished, then we scoot. After that, there's only the fashion show and then we're done for another year."

Lila grunted and played with her fork. The Academy had made some of the catering students provide the food for the luncheon. Rubbery chicken was not her idea of a tasty lunch. Thankfully, tea, coffee and hot chocolate were plentiful.

Edie leaned toward Xandie and Lila. "Is the luncheon always..."

"Boring as Hecate's toenails? Yep." Lila yawned and covered it with a hand.

"Emmaline's been unwell the last few days, but she was adamant we had to attend. Mildred has a day off. Thankfully." Edie forced a smile. "I get Great-Aunt duty."

"Hush, girl. One mustn't be rude." Emmaline glared at the three women and gestured to the podium where a pink-haired muse addressed the luncheon goers.

"We like to acknowledge all the contributions the late Britney Cygnus brought to Point Muse Academy. The Cygnus family has had a long connection to our educational institution and Britney served as a very successful P.T.A. president. But with a sad heart we must say farewell to her and welcome in her new official replacement, P.T.A. president Chloe Sylvis." The pink-haired woman stepped back and clapped loudly.

Chloe skipped to the podium and smiled at the crowd. "I would like to thank the alumni and the Academy for appointing me P.T.A. president. I will strive to be the best president ever." Chloe beamed at the crowd, waiting for the applause. She narrowed her gaze on the crowd as the silence dragged out and a few tables hurried into a frenzied clapping. Nodding, Chloe stepped down and sauntered past Emmaline, winking.

Emmaline straightened in her chair, her glare blistering.

"I don't think Emmaline likes Chloe very much," Edie whispered.

"I can hear you, Edith, and I think that certain people may have bitten off more than they can chew." Emmaline grimaced. "I need a tea. If you could fetch it?"

"Of course, Emmaline." Edie pushed her chair back and rushed toward the beverage table. She paused for a moment, then returned to the table. "They're out of your milk, but the server is positive there's more in the kitchen."

Emmaline shooed her great-niece away. "Do what you need to." The elderly woman sighed and drummed her nails on the table as she glared over at the victorious Chloe.

"You don't think Chloe will do a good job as president?" Lila considered the oldest Winchester. The woman put sour in a lemon and she definitely didn't approve of the bunny shifter.

"It's not my place to choose the president."

"But..."

"I feel she may not have had the Academy's best interests at heart. Or anyone else's interests but her own."

Wow, say it like you mean it. "I'm sure everything will work out the way it's supposed to."

Edie joined them and carefully placed a milky tea in front of her great-aunt. "Sorry it took so long. I had issues tracking down your milk. But I eventually found an open one in the fridge."

Emmaline sniffed and took a sip of tea. She nodded at her niece. "Tolerable." She continued to sip as others chattered around her.

Edie checked her watch. "Mildred was supposed to have a full day, but apparently has decided to only take half. She should be here any minute to look after Emmaline."

"She does seem devoted to your Great-Aunt," Xandie offered.

"Obsessed more like," Lila muttered under her breath. Edie and Xandie froze, and Lila sighed. "She's right behind me, isn't she?"

"She's the cat's mother, Lila Harrow."

Lila turned and confronted the glowering house-keeper. "Lovely to see you, Mildred. Enjoy your morning off?"

Mildred glared at Lila. "That Harrow mouth…" Her words stuttered to a halt as Emmaline dropped her cup on the table with a clatter, milky tea spreading across the tablecloth.

The elderly woman grabbed her throat, cough-ing. Frantic eyes met her niece's and she reached out, pointing at Edie before she bent over and retched continuously.

Mildred scooted the wheelchair out from the table and bent over her employer. She rubbed her back and whispered something before straightening.

Emmaline groaned and vomited. She held her stomach, moaning.

Edie wrung her hands. "I need to get Emmaline to the hospital."

The elderly woman shook her head and pointed at the tea, all the while moaning.

Mildred grabbed the handles of the wheelchair. "Ms. Winchester can't stand hospitals. She has a private healer; they'll meet her at Winchester House. I will deal with her." Ignoring Edie protests, Mildred wheeled her moaning charge out of the hall.

Chloe Sylvis stepped up, arms crossed. "Leave it to Emmaline Winchester to make a memorable exit and disrupt my presidential swearing in."

Edie fisted her hands. "You make it sound like she got sick on purpose."

"If the wheelchair fits..." Chloe winked and wandered off back to her table.

The bunny shifter seemed pretty sure Emmaline had timed getting sick just to disrupt Chloe's limelight. But considering two murders had occurred in a week and Lila had been attacked by a Lamia, maybe it wasn't a coincidence or an accident that Emmaline had fallen sick. Lila stared at the spreading spot of spilt milky tea. She leaned over and sniffed, withdrawing from the slightly bitter smell. She snagged Xandie. "You need to call your bear boyfriend and make sure he tests Emmaline's tea. Meanwhile, I'll take Edie back to Winchester House to check on Emmaline."

"Why does my police chief need to test spilt tea?"

"Because I think Emmaline may have been poisoned." And after the way Chloe had winked and smirked at the elderly Winchester, the bunny shifter was top of the suspect list.

Actually, Chloe Sylvis was the only name on the list.

TWELVE

"Thanks for bringing me home, Lila. I'm sure Mildred would have come back for me after the healer checked Emmaline out." Edie unlocked the large Victorian front door and let them both into the entranceway of Winchester House.

"I doubt that," Lila muttered. She peered around the wood-paneled entrance way. Multiple doorways led off from the hallway. Heavy furniture and fussy antiques filled what she could see of the other rooms.

Edie paced then turned to Lila. "I'll just pop upstairs and check on Emmaline. Feel free to have a look around." Edie left Lila without another word and bounded upstairs.

Taking Edie at her word, Lila wandered around the bottom level of Winchester House. Heavy burgundy curtains protected the interior of the house from the sun, and dark paneling added to the gloom. The house sported a three-season porch, a living room, parlor, sunroom and a large kitchen all painted an unappealing gray that matched the outside.

"Thank the witches for Harrow House. Nothing bland or gloomy in sight." Because of generations of Harrow witches practicing the craft, Harrow House definitely had a stubborn personality of its own. "Winchester House on the other hand feels soulless."

Raised voices from upstairs caught Lila's attention and she drifted closer to the stairs, pretending not to eavesdrop.

"I have every right to see her. She's family. I just want to know she's okay. That's all."

"Ms. Winchester herself has asked for no visitors, and that includes yourself. The healer is with her and she'll recover better if she's not disturbed."

Mildred's frosty tones carried clearly downstairs to Lila.

Edie blew out a loud breath. "Fine, just tell my aunt I asked after her. If she needs me to do anything for her, let me know."

"You've done enough, don't you think?"

The door slammed and Edie trudged down the heavy wooden stairs. She paused at the bottom when she spotted Lila watching and mustered a weak smile. "Aunt Emmaline's doing okay. She has the healer in there and Mildred's with her right now."

Lila cleared her throat. "I heard." Mildred was beyond overprotective of her employer and seemed to think Edie had something to do with her aunt's poisoning.

"Mildred has worked for my Great-Aunt since she was a young woman. She's devoted to Emmaline."

"And she's suspicious of you?"

Changing the subject, Edie gestured for Lila to follow her. "Would you like a tour of the outside? It's prettier than the inside."

Lila nodded, and Edie led her through a sunroom to a beautiful, landscaped fieldstone terrace. Glancing back at the house, Edie let out a deep breath.

"Feel better?"

"Always feels like someone's watching and judging me in there," Edie admitted.

"Mildred probably is." Lila encouraged Edie to keep talking. "Show me the gardens. Aren't the Winchesters green witches?"

Edie brightened. "Most of us are. My skills are pretty basic, but I like growing herbs."

"And Emmaline?"

"From what I gather, her skills lay in herbs as well, but since she's in a wheelchair, I don't think she gets out too much anymore. Even her greenhouses are locked up tight." Edie pointed to a small ancient-looking stone and glass greenhouse that lay at the end of a granite path. "Winchester House gardens were designed and landscaped by different genera-tions. Aunt Emmaline gets an external gardener in every so often to keep up the tidiness now she can't garden."

Lila slowly turned and gazed around. Honestly, the garden was lovely. An old stone boundary fence with overgrown moss creeping over it circled the property. Clumps of oaks, along with shrub roses and what looked like blueberries, dotted the landscape. A meandering paved path wandered under a pretty wooden arch. Raised flowerbeds and well-groomed hedges completed the idyllic view.

Edie stood near a heavy, white-painted arch and rapped a knuckle on the wood. "A post and beam arbor made with Douglas Fir. The Winchesters built things to last." Edie pointed to the oak trees that dotted the back of the property. "Vaccinium Angus-tifolium, wild low bush blueberries. Most of the plants in the garden are long-bloom annuals." Edie strode over to a small walled area with a wooden door. "This is the herb garden. Mostly herbs and edible flowers in here now. There's even a little shed for starting seedlings." Edie appeared animated, her earlier discomfort from the way Mildred treated her completely dissipated.

"So, what herbs do you grow here?" Lila waggled her eyebrows. "The odd witchy herb?"

"Emmaline isn't Elspeth Harrow." Edie giggled. "I didn't plant anything, but it's mainly basil, oregano, mint, thyme, rosemary, lavender and edible flowers like lemon jam marigolds and nasturtiums."

"Elspeth would be disappointed." Lila sat on an ornate metal chair, with Edie following suit. "Your grandmother was Emmaline's sister?"

"Emmaline was quite a bit older than my grandmother, Eudalia, and they weren't close. Her parents sent my grandmother away for schooling when she was very young."

"No Academy?"

"Nope. My grandmother never mentioned why Emmaline was sent to the Academy while she attended boarding school. But I do know as soon as my grandmother could, she married and left town. She never wanted anything to do with her parents or her sister."

"Another family feud?" Point Muse seemed to have been founded on feuding plans.

"Who knows? My grandmother never spoke of her family. That's why I was interested in visiting Point Muse after she passed away. But Emmaline hasn't exactly been welcoming."

Lila snorted. "Yeah, I can see that." She paused for a moment, but decided to carry on, subtlety be damned. "What did Mildred mean when she said you'd done enough?"

"I served the tea to Emmaline. I keep snakes and my green witch skills aren't as great as the rest of the Winchesters." Edie sagged. "I have a pretty strong feeling she's fingered me as the killer and is insinuating that I tried to poison Emmaline. Probably thinks I'm after the Winchester House and the non-existent family wealth."

"Well, the house is... It's..." Lila tried to find an appropriate descriptor for the lackluster, uninspired house.

"It's old-fashioned, gloomy and depressing, except for the garden. I really don't want this house. I just want to go home now. No wonder my grandmother avoided any mention of her family."

"She never mentioned Emmaline or Point Muse at all?"

"Not really. Except..."

"What?" Talk about being on tenterhooks. Lila nodded encouragingly.

"Toward the end, just before my grandmother died, she rambled a little. All she really said about her family was that they had dark times and that she was glad she'd left and hoped we'd all escaped the troubles."

Lila bit her lip. "Escaped the troubles? Interesting choice of words." What kind of troubles would the Winchesters have had that qualified as dark times?

"Speaking of troubles," Edie muttered and jerked her head.

Lila turned in her chair and peered over the back of the seat.

Mildred, steel spine and stout body, stomped toward them. The only thing surprising about her appearance was the gloating smirk that graced her dour face and the presence of Police Chief Zach Braun looming behind her.

The bear shifter nodded his thanks to the housekeeper then focused on Lila and Edie. "Sorry to interrupt you, but I'm afraid I need to speak to Edith Winchester."

Lila waved a welcoming hand to the chief. "Feel free to pull up a chair, we're just gossiping."

"I'm afraid I have to speak with Ms. Winchester in a more formal setting." He focused on Edie. "It would be better for your case if you came in voluntarily."

Edie exchanged a wide-eyed glance with Lila. "You're arresting me?"

Braun held up a hand. "At this stage, you are not under arrest, but I do need to formally interview you."

Swallowing hard, Edie stood and pasted on a brave face. "Thanks for being here, Lila. I really appreciated it."

Lila snorted. "If you think I'll let you head to the pokey by yourself, you're crazy." She stood and glared at Braun. "Hope you enjoyed the honey buns. It'll be a long while before you see any more, Zach Braun."

Sighing, the police chief gestured to the women. "After you, ladies."

Lila raised her nose in the air and crowded next to Edie as they marched through the gloomy Winchester House.

Mildred stood with arms crossed in the front hallway, the door wide open. She wrinkled her nose as the two passed by as if she'd smelt something rotten.

The women exited and stood on the front porch, waiting for Braun to join them. The heavy wooden door slammed shut behind the trio.

"I have a feeling I've out-stayed my welcome," Edie muttered.

Curtains twitching in the upper story of Winchester House grabbed Lila's attention. Someone was definitely keeping a close eye on Edie Winchester.

Maybe Lila should too.

"I told you. I have no clue how the ipecac syrup got into Emmaline's tea. I didn't put it there. Why would I make my Great-Aunt sick? She's old, it could have killed her."

"Exactly. Winchester House is a historical land-mark on a large portion of land within town limits. It's probably worth a pretty penny."

"Sorry?"

"You're her great-niece, Emmaline's an elderly woman, maybe you're thinking you'll inherit?"

Edie snorted. "And she can't stand me. It's more

likely Mildred will be left the house than I will. Besides, I wouldn't hurt her, I wouldn't hurt anyone."

"Uh huh." Braun stared at Edie before opening a folder and showing her a picture of leafy green plants. "Know what this is?"

Taking the photo, Edie frowned at it. "Just because I'm a green witch, doesn't mean I know every plant in the world."

"How about the ones in your own garden?" Braun gently took the photo from Edie and tapped the image. "My experts tell me it's Ipecacuanha and its roots are used for syrup of ipecac. And it was found in your garden."

"Not my house. Not my garden. I had no clue it was there. I've been here a week or so. Obviously, it was planted before I got here." Edie sat back, glowering at the chief of police.

"Have you ever visited here before? Maybe a little while ago and didn't tell anyone? In the end, you might not have planted it, but you definitely could have used it to make your Great-Aunt sick."

"I made her a cup of tea with the milk I found in the kitchen. I did not at any stage poison her tea to make Emmaline sick." Edie leaned forward and pointed a finger at Braun. "And before you ask, I did not kill anyone else either. I barely know anyone in town." She shook her head. "No wonder my grandmother ran away from Point Muse."

"You won't be going anywhere just yet." Braun gathered paperwork and stood. "You need to take this seriously, Ms. Winchester."

The door to the interview room slammed open and Lila stood framed in the doorway. "That's enough, copper. My client has answered all your questions adequately. You have no choice but to release her."

"Client? You're a baker, not a lawyer, Lila."

Lila glowered at Braun. "Exactly. The bakery is like a bartender or a hairdresser or a mental health person. People tell us things, and we help them feel better."

"Good feelings do not equate to a law degree. And they certainly aren't getting Ms. Winchester off the hook of an attempted murder charge."

"Since all you have is circumstantial evidence, you have nothing to charge her with. Release her." Lila winked at Edie. "Why don't we ask the person in question? Edie, do you want me to represent you?"

"Yep. Definitely. That would be great." Edie sat up straight and smoothed her flyway red hair. "Lila

Harrow's my representative. Any more questions, please direct them to her."

Braun slapped the file against his leg. "This isn't legal. You're not qualified to represent Ms. Winchester on any legal matter."

"I have something better than legal qualifications." Lila smirked at Braun, then reached out and dragged Aggie Braun in front of her. Lila poked her head around the bear shifter. "I have your mother."

"Zachary Braun. Release Edie right now," Aggie Braun, bear shifter, police dispatcher and Zach's mother, growled at her son. Her furry mono brow twitched. "We both know your evidence is circumstantial at best. Release Edie into Lila's custody. I'm sure she'll take responsibility for Ms. Winchester."

"Yes ma'am." Zack sighed. "I never win when you all gang up on me." He jerked his head at Edie. "Get out of here, Winchester. Don't leave town and watch your back." Braun stepped around his mother and shot Lila the evil eye. "Low blow bringing my mother into this, but I guess it could've been worse."

"I could've bought Elspeth." Her grandmother had a pathological aversion to law enforcement. Any excuse to break someone out of the pokey and Elspeth would be upfront and present, smoke bomb in hand.

"Thanks, Lila. I appreciate your help." Edie stood and smiled gratefully at the baker.

"Don't thank me, thank parental manipulation."

Aggie winked at the girls. "Guilting your kids is a parent's right. Now skedaddle back to that bakery, I have a powerful hankering for honey cake."

"You got it, Aggie." Lila dragged Edie out of the interview room. The bakery was a good idea.

Nothing like baking while puzzling out a murderer's identity…

THIRTEEN

"Our little bird has flown the jailhouse coop." Elspeth strode into the bakery, rocking a fire engine red mohawk wig. Colin followed closely behind with a matching little hat with its own red mohawk attached.

"In your punk phase, I see." Lila placed a plate of tiny lemon cakes on the table in front of Edie and Holly.

"Always stand out, never blend in… Unless you're conducting nefarious schemes." Elspeth winked at the room before settling herself into a chair next to Edie. "How was your first experience of police interrogation? You gotta watch out for the fuzz, they're sneaky."

Edie mustered a small smile. "It wasn't too bad.

Chief Braun is pretty fair, but I guess the evidence is kind of piling up against me."

"Purely circumstantial. No substance. Just ignore the police, that's what we do." Lila nodded for Hester to take over the bakery counter and joined the table.

"It's not so easy when you're the number one suspect."

"Chin up girl. Eat one of Lila's sugar concoctions. Gratuitous amounts of sugar always make me feel better."

Lila offered Edie the plate of cakes. "I'd take Elspeth's advice. *'Sunshine for the Soul'* cupcakes. A special blend of mine. Will definitely make you feel better." Lila didn't have any flashy Harrow gifts, but her magic-infused baking was out of this world. The one thing she could count on was her ability to make people feel good with sugar.

Edie took a cake and nibbled the side. Then she perked up and took a larger bite. "That's amazing, like liquid sunshine."

"Sweet cheeks has a gift, she just refuses to share sometimes." Colin sat behind Elspeth's chair and shot Lila a grumpy glare.

"I told you. Sweet food all the time isn't good for

you." Lila shifted the plate of goodies further away from Colin.

"What are you? The sugar police? Or are you channeling your mother?" Colin hit back.

"*Oooo.* Burn," Holly snickered at the aghast expression on her cousin's face.

"What a truly horrible insult." The last person Lila wanted to mimic was her no-nonsense, empath veterinarian mother.

"I taught him everything I know," Elspeth cackled and Lila's old-fashioned bakery till clicked and clattered, with the money drawer shooting open and closed.

"Tone it down, hag. This is my place of work." Lila glared at her grandmother.

"Killjoy. No fun at all."

The kitchen door swung open and Matthew Grim and Nash, Lila's hellhound, trotted out.

Both had icing smeared on their faces.

Colin booed at the cake munching duo. "Favoritism. You let the puppy eat cakes. I say cakes for everyone."

"Oops." Matthew wiped his face with the back of his hand. "That's my fault. Hester said I could have a snack, so I thought I'd share with the puppy."

Nash bounded up to Colin and tried to squeeze in next to him, but Colin turned his

back on the hellhound. "No love for the cake eating puppy."

Whining, Nash nudged Colin. When the pug refused to look at him, the puppy

stared hard at the cakes. The food rose into the air, wobbling until it stabilized, before shooting off toward Colin. When the plate settled on the ground, Nash pushed the cakes over to the pug.

Colin cracked an eye open, then sniffed. "I'll take this as my due for being a maligned

pug. We may now commence friendship again as long as you don't expect me to share." He dumped his face into the middle of the plate and hoovered the cakes down.

"That is the most disgusting sight I have ever seen. Surely that's against health and safety laws." Chloe Sylvis, followed by her teenage daughter, Marion, stepped into the bakery. "I don't know what's worse. The animal bathing in icing or having a murderer take tea with the rest of Point Muse." The curvy bunny shifter wrinkled her nose.

Lila glared at the pretentious P.T.A. president.

"You don't like what you see here, go somewhere else for your caffeine hit."

"Now, now, Harrow. Don't be so sensitive. You're a business owner, you need to be able to take the odd criticism."

"Mom." Marion tugged in her mother's arm. "Can't we just get the order to go?"

Chloe patted her daughter's hand. "Of course, sweetie. Why don't you put our order in with the Brownie, while I chat with Lila?"

Sighing, Marion trudged off and ordered the cappuccinos to go in a low voice.

Her cornflower blue eyes projecting innocence, Chloe strode further into the bakery. "I must admit, Edie, I'm very surprised to see you out and about. I would have thought that Chief Braun would've locked you up tight by now."

Putting down the cake she'd nibbled on, Edie dusted her hands off without meeting Chloe's gaze. "Chief Braun just questioned me. He knows I didn't hurt anyone."

"Really?" Chloe tapped her fingers on her chin, deep in thought. "From what I hear, the evidence is starting to mount up and goodness knows your family has motive." She trilled a laugh. "It's always the quiet ones, isn't it?"

That sneaky bunny knew something and itched to rub everyone's noses in it. "Spit out whatever you want to say, Sylvis. We don't have all day. I've got mean girl memes to post on Witchbook," Lila sneered.

"I have no clue what you mean, Lila. I'm just here for a drink." Chloe deposited herself at a table next to Lila's and shoved her handbag under the chair. She traced a fingernail along the table surface. "I'm just saying the issues in town started when poor Edie came to visit. Emmaline must be so over-whelmed with the stain brought upon the honorable Winchester name."

Colin wandered over to Chloe and disappeared under her chair for a few moments before reap-pearing with a satisfied smirk. He quickly hotfooted it back into the kitchen, followed by Nash.

"Ms. Sylvis, Edie hasn't been formally charged with any crime and as such you are just speculating. And that doesn't help anyone." Matthew stepped up next to Lila's chair and frowned at the gossipy bunny.

Way to go, reaper, Lila silently crowed in support of her intimidating tenant. Matthew's steely gray eyes and heavy brows screamed don't mess with me.

Lila cocked an eyebrow at the bunny and waited for her response.

Flustered by the reaper's involvement, Chloe smoothed her hair. "Of course, if you say so, Mr. Grim." She flashed a bright smile. "I mean, you *are* the expert. I heard you have to share an office here. The Sylvis family has plenty of contacts. I have no doubt I could find you private office space." She fluttered her eyebrows at the man.

Flirting? In front of her with... Lila's brain blanked, and she stood, her chair scooting out behind her, hitting Grim.

Matthew sidestepped the chair. "Thank you for the offer. I'll keep it in mind."

"Excuse me?" Lila spun and hissed at Matthew, hands on her hips, "After I offered you a place in my bakery, you desert me for a man-eating bunny?"

"I appropriated the space, you never actually offered anything."

"No baked goods for you." Honestly, one bat of the eyelashes and the reaper abandoned ship for a predator bunny.

"It's better than Witch Island. So much drama." Elspeth munched on a box of popcorn she'd scrounged from somewhere.

"Is little old me causing friction?" Chloe cooed.

"I just wanted to help the poor reaper out. So much drama in town right now."

Lila turned her back on the traitor and focused on Chloe, little Miss mean girl. "How much drama is caused by you?"

Chloe looked surprised. "None. This is all someone else's meddling. I'm just reaping the benefits. Get it? Reaping?" Chloe tittered into her hand.

"Mom? Can we go now? Remember that appointment?" Marion offered her mother her cappuccino. "We need to get going. If you want to make it." The teenager widened her eyes and jerked her head meaningfully.

"Quite right." Chloe stood and grabbed her bag. "Can't miss such an important meeting." She winked at Edie. "Don't worry, little Winchester. I'm sure everything will resolve itself sooner rather than later. See you at the fashion show." She finger waved and strode out the door with her daughter behind her.

Lila stood to close the door behind them but paused as she heard the duo arguing.

"Seriously, Mom. The mean girl routine is pointless. Focus on your meeting. That's more important."

"Crushing your rivals is always important, but you're right. The meeting takes precedent. I *will* get my way and there's nothing anyone can do unless they want dirty laundry aired." Chloe smiled, blinding white teeth on show.

"Quit gloating, Mother. It freaks me out."

Chloe handed Marion her drink. "Hold this for a moment, I have to check my make-up. One must always look the best when they defeat the competition." The bunny shifter opened her bag and rummaged through the contents before letting out an ungodly scream as she withdrew a sloppy cake-covered hand.

Lila quickly closed the bakery door and flipped the sign to closed.

"What's wrong?" Holly frowned and pointed to the door. "Since when do you close early?"

Taking a step away from the door, Lila refused to turn and look at the still screaming Chloe. "Since someone deposited regurgitated yellow cakes in Chloe's handbag, predator bunny is on a rampage."

Colin poked his head out of the kitchen and cleared his throat. "Sometimes a pug's got to clean his innards. The bag seemed like the perfect place for a deposit." The dog shrugged, unconcerned.

"Chloe wouldn't agree." Edie blinked furiously for a few seconds, before losing the fight. She subsided into a chair with belly-shaking laughter. "I don't mean to be rude, but that's priceless."

"Life with Harrows can get messy." Elspeth shrugged. "Besides, couldn't happen to a nicer person."

Considering the classic mean girl scenario that had just played out in her bakery, Lila couldn't fault Elspeth's words. The whole episode raised Lila's hackles. Chloe acted victorious, like she'd won the war and defeated her opponent. Could her mysterious meeting have something to do with her gloating? Just what did the rabid bunny shifter have planned? Making a split-second decision, Lila motioned to Edie. "Come on, Winchester. Let's get you home so you can check on your Great-Aunt."

Edie jumped up. "That would be great. Thanks, Lila.

The two women marched to the kitchen, but Lila paused and swung around, pointing at the reaper. "Don't think I haven't forgotten your flirting with maniac Barbie bunny. We *will* have words later." They weren't actually dating, but that didn't stop her from pointing out the reaper's wrongdoings. And she had to get Edie back home and figure out just what Chloe Sylvis had planned.

Piece of cake for a witchy baker sleuth.

FOURTEEN

"I don't think that's a good sign." Lila pointed to the two baby-pink suitcases with Edie's name printed on the side where they lay in the hallway.

"They're mine." Edie frowned and glanced around the otherwise empty hallway.

A muffled cough sounded from the library. Lila nodded to Edie and they converged on the room.

Lila swung the door open and stepped in. The only occupant of the room, a blanket-covered Emmaline, sat in her wheelchair, facing the door.

"I see the Chief has released you." Distaste dripped from Emmaline's every word.

Storm warning alert. "He had very little evidence against Edie, which isn't surprising, since she's innocent."

"It doesn't matter if she's innocent. The damage is already done to the Winchester name," Emmaline spat out.

Edie quivered and wrapped her arms around her waist. "I truly didn't hurt you or anyone. I'm innocent."

"But the chief of police took you in for questioning. My neighbors saw the police car parked out front while he took my statement. People saw you taken into the police station." Emmaline slapped the armrest of her wheelchair. "The damage to the family name is unacceptable. After everything I have done, I will not tolerate the smear on our family. I want you to leave." The Winchester matriarch pointed imperiously to the bags in the hallway.

Biting her lip, Edie nodded. "I can understand you feeling that way, Great-Aunt Emmaline, but I truly didn't hurt anyone. I just wanted to get to know you."

"And now we're done."

"I'll make sure there's nothing left in my room, then I'll be out of your hair." Edie shuffled to the door and disappeared upstairs.

"Wow, you're a real grouch, Emmaline. Oscar could take lessons from you." At the elderly woman's baffled face, Lila explained. "Oscar the Grouch from

Sesame Street. He is stone cold mean and pushes everyone away, just like you did to Edie."

"My family is not your business, Ms. Harrow." The elderly woman plucked at her blanket fretfully.

"It is my business and she's your family. She looked forward to meeting you. Edie wanted to conncct with the last of her family after her grandmother died. Your sister, remember?"

"Eudalia," Emmaline growled her sister's name. "Pampered little princess who got to leave Point Muse and live a normal life."

"Is that why you're kicking Edie out? Because you hated your sister?"

The energy drained out of Emmaline and she settled back into her wheelchair. "I didn't hate my sister, but everything came easy to her. Life, love, everything."

Bitter much? "Edie said her grandmother refused to talk about her family or Point Muse. At least, until she was on her deathbed."

Emmaline froze. "Her mutterings mean nothing to me."

Lila strolled around the room and let her fingers drift over the shelves. From the corner of her eyes, she saw the old woman stiffen and then relax. Looks like they had an old-fashioned game of hot and cold.

"Her grandmother said her family had dark days and she hoped her child and grandchild had escaped the troubles. Any idea what she meant?"

"Eudalia had a dramatic streak. Came from being our parents' favorite, I suspect. She spoke nonsense most of the time."

Slowing her pace around the room even further, Lila watched her quarry's body language until Emmaline became a stone statue as Lila drew level with a bookcase. "Eudalia was on her deathbed when she told Edie that. I'm pretty sure she was beyond dramatics."

Emmaline gripped her wheelchair armrests. "I doubt that. Shouldn't you go look for Edith?"

"Trying to get rid of me?" Lila turned her attention to the bookcase. She ran her hand over the shelves filled with leather bound books. "I love the smell of old books, don't you? All those literary gems hidden away. Just makes you want to stop for awhile. Maybe I should have been the Librarian."

Lila focused on a shelf in front of her as she spotted something metallic wedged behind a text on treaties of magical familiars. She carefully drew out a tarnished silver frame, featuring a decades younger Emmaline and a tall blonde-headed man, standing close together. Lila knew she'd hit pay dirt when

Emmaline let out an audible gasp. Lila held the photo out. "Someone important?"

All color drained from the elderly woman's face and reconstituted itself in her red-knuckled grip on the armrests of her wheelchair.

"That is not your business. That's my private property."

Pay dirt. Ms. Winchester seemed freaked out, which meant whatever the man's identity, he was important to Emmaline. "Funny thing. There's a rumor in town that someone disappeared years ago with a Cygnus man, but he died tragically only a few weeks later." Lila tapped the photo. "That's him, isn't it?"

Emmaline's hands shook as she made an effort to release her grip on her wheelchair. "You're invading my privacy and digging up old hurts."

Lila sighed, crossed over to Emmaline and crouched in front of her. She held up the photo. "It's never good to have secrets, they have a way of coming back and hexing you in the butt."

The elderly woman snorted. "You could be right." She reached out a knobby hand and gently tugged the photo frame out of Lila's hands. "Such a good-looking man with a kind heart to go with it. Unusual for the Cygnus clan."

A deep dark Winchester secret. Understanding clicked into place. "You eloped?"

"Our families weren't happy with our association." Emmaline sniffed disdainfully. "The Winchester name is an old respected one, and the Cygnus clan did not have such an established reputation before Point Muse."

"Your parents didn't approve?"

"No. But we thought we knew best. Tempestuous youth and all that." Emmaline raised eyes that welled with tears. "Donald and I loved each other. He said he could overcome anything." She traced the outline of her husband's face.

Emmaline didn't normally engender sympathy in anyone who came across her, but the grief Lila saw in the woman couldn't be faked. "What happened?"

"He loved the water, wanted a honeymoon near the sea. We went boating, but a sudden storm blew in. Donald thought he could handle it." Emmaline handed the frame back to Lila. "But he couldn't. We tipped into the water. I think he banged his head. I tried looking for him, but I couldn't find a trace. I managed to get back to shore and notify the authorities. They searched but found nothing. Eventually, I returned home to my loving parents." Emmaline's dry tone indicated her parents' reaction had been anything but loving.

"And the Cygnus family?"

"Thought I had murdered him at worst, and at best, failed to help him as he drowned. My parents decided I should retire from society for a while. I agreed happily, I had no desire to see the Cygnus or Sylvis clan's enmity for me."

"Cygnus I can understand, but why Sylvis?"

Emmaline settled the blanket tighter around herself. "Before Donald and I eloped, he'd been engaged to Louella Sylvis. A family match meant to end the feud and cement a business alliance in potions and poisons."

"Donald dumped the bunny for a Winchester."

"Exactly. Neither side forgave the other and of course, the Winchester name suffered for a while."

"The Winchester name. Is that why you asked Edie to leave? The damage to the Winchester reputation?"

"The Winchesters are an important part of Point Muse history. Having a murder suspect connected to the Winchester family is not the legacy I want to leave."

Righteous old bat. "Edie hasn't hurt anyone. She's your great niece. She doesn't deserve this."

"This is still my house, Lila Harrow. And it's my choice who lives here. It's safer if Edith Winchester removes herself from my vicinity." Emmaline slapped her wheelchair, red flashing into her pallid cheeks.

"Safe for who, Emmaline? You or her?"

"How dare you."

The library door swung open and Mildred, the Winchester housekeeper, stood framed in the doorway. "I think it's time you left, Ms. Harrow. Ms. Winchester needs her rest."

Edie pushed past Mildred with a small bag clasped in her arms. "I'm really sorry about everything that's happened. I had nothing to do with the murders or your poisoning, but I can understand you being upset. I'm grateful to have met you at least." Edie waited for Emmaline to respond, but her great-aunt just turned her head and stared out the window.

Lila took charge and ushered Edie out into the hallway, ignoring Mildred's grunts as they shoved past her.

Mildred slammed the library door shut behind them.

Hefting the two suitcases, Lila winked at Edie.

"Come on, Winchester. Let's get you out of this mausoleum."

Edie sighed as she stepped outside into the late afternoon sun. "I'm kinda glad to be out of there, even if I am homeless."

"Please, what kind of Harrow would I be if I didn't offer you a place to stay?"

"I can't impose on you, Lila. You barely know me."

Lila snorted. "You're doing me a favor. My family dragged me to Harrow House after I was attacked. If I invite you to stay at my apartment it means I get to move home too. Safety in numbers and all that."

"Are you sure? I mean, I'm a murder suspect."

"We both know you aren't a murderer. Now hurry up. I feel a pizza party coming on." Lila trudged to her bakery van, Edie following behind.

Gratuitous amounts of carbs and dairy was exactly what she needed to plan her next move.

A move that might put her one step ahead of a killer... *Hopefully.*

"What is it about a double pepperoni pizza that makes you feel so good?" Lila lounged back on her couch with a happy sigh. She picked off a slice of pepperoni and flipped it over to Nash. "Don't ever say I don't share, hound."

"Pizza," Nash growled, then snatched the pizza topping out of the air.

"That can't be good for him. Shouldn't he eat doggy food?" Holly grimaced and moved away from the hellhound as he stood drooling, staring at her slice of pizza.

"He's a hellhound. I'm pretty sure pizza toppings can't hurt him." Xandie flicked a piece of pineapple at Holly. "Besides, you're the one who wanted pineapple on the pizza. That combination has to be more deadly than a piece of pepperoni."

Holly poked a pineapple-covered tongue at her cousin.

"Do you squabble like this all the time?" Edie nibbled on a slice of plain cheese pizza.

Lila swallowed a mouthful of pizza. "Pretty much."

"It's our version of bonding," Xandie agreed.

"They just like picking on me," Holly whined.

"The whole family is exactly the same. They

thrive on drama." Matthew leaned closer to Lila and snagged a slice of pizza off her plate.

"That's the last slice of pepperoni," Lila complained while she attempted to ignore the fact the hunky reaper sat plastered against her side on the couch.

"Not my fault you took the last piece. You need to share, Harrow."

"And you need to scoot over, you mammoth." Lila wiggled and glared at Matthew. The side of her thigh pressed against him and she wiggled again to dispel the feeling of warmth seeping along her leg.

"Ants in your pants, Lila? Did Elspeth hex you again?" Xandie shot a knowing smile at her cousin. "Payback's a witch, cuz."

Holly glanced between the two cousins. "What? Did I miss something?"

Lila glared at the room. "You missed nothing but an invasion of space and privacy." "And denial's a river in Egypt." Xandie winked.

Matthew choked on his mouthful of pizza and thumped his chest a few times before clearing his airways. "This family is never boring. Even with their bad luck, still entertaining."

Edie placed a slice of pizza down on her plate. "What bad luck?"

"Corpses," Lila said bluntly. "We don't make them, but we definitely find them."

"Maybe I have that bad luck too."

"It's okay, Edie. That's why we're here. Between all of us Harrows and even an annoying reaper, we'll find the killer and clear your name."

Nash padded over to Edie and laid his head on her lap, whining softly until she rubbed his ears.

"See?" Lila pointed out. "Nash is a dreaded hellhound. If you were a nefarious killer, he'd have sniffed you out already. All we have to do is keep the cops off your back and present them with another viable suspect." Hopefully, Edie believed her.

Grim raised a hand. "You've forgotten one more thing."

"What?" all three cousins chimed in together.

"You have to survive the Academy's final event... *The fashion show.*"

Blood rushed from Lila's face to her hands, leaving a trail of fire behind. *The fashion show.* Elspeth's favorite event. One she never failed to disrupt with chaos and mayhem.

Maybe spending a day in jail wasn't a bad idea.

FIFTEEN

"What fresh hell is this?" Lila covered her eyes and moaned. "Seriously, this might affect my eyes." She peeked through her fingers, shuddered and closed her eyes again.

Holly pried Lila's fingers away from her face. "It's not that bad. The kids tried really hard. Stop being so judgmental."

Lila lowered her hands and took a breath. "Fine, the fashion students of Point Muse Academy have turned out a fine example of fashion throughout the decades, honoring the Academy's Founding Day celebrations."

Xandie looked sideways at her cousin. "That was strangely formal and specific."

"That's what the Point Muse Chronicles will report in tomorrow's edition."

Holly's eyes grew wide. "Have you developed psychic gifts you haven't told us about?"

"Wow, you are gullible." Lila shook her head. "That's what the Chronicle reports every year. The Academy are sponsors for Percy's newspaper. Unless it's hot news, he just trots out the same copy every year." Percival Hague, a.k.a. Percy, had helped out Xandie when Zach Braun's clingy ex-girlfriend had been killed and the murderer had tried to frame the bear shifter. Percy was the head reporter...*make that the only reporter*.

"Shoot. Being a psychic would have rocked." Holly turned her glum face to the catwalk and winced. "You know, now that I have a closer look, the designs really are bad. And bright, really bright."

Lila winked as a particularly eye-blinding neon green fought with a putrid eggplant purple color in the guise of the hooded cape paired with a strange, button-down pinafore. She squinted with one eye closed. "At least the clothing is well-made. It could be worse. We could have a wardrobe malfunction."

"Heads up. Mean bunny alert." Holly nudged Lila and pointed to the runway.

Chloe and Marion Sylvis pranced down the

makeshift runway holding hands, wearing matching fuchsia corsets and bustled skirts. The duo sashayed along the runway, both mother and daughter, then split and headed to opposite ends, standing still and cocking their hips out to one side in a classic model pose.

"Are they alive? Are they some kind of fashion bots? I don't think they're even blinking." Lila shuddered. There was something unnatural about matching mother-daughter poses and outfits.

"It's off-putting, but not as much as the cone bra on that little blonde's head." Holly pointed to a teenager in a powder blue tracksuit. The girl strutted down the runway, pausing to blow kisses every few meters. A pale cream kitten pattered behind the girl with another cone bra tight around his head.

"Seriously, Elspeth? What part of mayhem did you not get?" So much for Elspeth's promises, but Lila did admit her grandmother rocked her cone bra headgear.

"I thought you said she promised to behave?" Holly hissed.

Lila shrugged. "It's Elspeth. When has she ever behaved in public?"

Chloe and Marion Sylvis moved closer together, frowning at the lack of attention from the crowd.

Spotting something behind them, Marion tugged on her mother's arm and spun her around until she faced the fashion interloper.

"Get off my stage," Chloe shrieked. "How dare you?"

The cone bra model pranced past the matching duo and stopped at the end of the runway. Her eyes sparkled as she posed one way, then another, mimicking the bunny shifters' actions.

Screeching, Chloe grabbed the model's arm and wrenched her around. "This is my fashion show. My school. I'm the P.T.A. president. I demand you cease and desist immediately, or I'll have you locked up."

Lila covered her eyes. "Don't mention the cops."

"Not the cops." Holly covered her mouth as the teenager bellowed and shook off Chloe's clawed hand.

Xandie covered her ears. "The cops tipped her over."

"The fuzz won't take me alive, suckers." The girl grabbed a small balloon out of her pocket and smashed it at her feet. Bright pink smoke bubbled out and swiftly covered the fashion show stage.

"Hang on, toots. I got your back." The pale cream kitten barreled into the smoke, cone bra hanging lopsided off its head like a bizarre underwear helmet. The cat ploughed into Chloe, knocking her down onto all fours. Her daughter took a prudent couple of steps back. The cat backed away and turned, presenting a fuzzy tale in Chloe's face. The feline waggled for a few seconds before sagging. "Take that, fashion rabbit. In your face. *Literally.*"

Chloe's face turned green and she slapped a hand to her nose and mouth. Dry heaves wracked her frame.

"She fed him tuna." Xandie stared, horrified, as various members of the P.T.A. rushed onto the stage to protect the president.

"Yep. She primed the pump. Devious and deadly masterstroke. All aimed at a quick getaway." Lila pointed to the still teenage-looking Elspeth and her feline making their escape out an exit.

"I think we need to make a quick escape too." Holly pointed to a trio of bright haired muses heading their way.

"I think you're right." Lila slipped out of her aisle chair and crouched low, scuttling to the back wall, Xandie and Holly following.

"Why aren't we heading for an exit? We'll be trapped in here," Xandie hissed.

Lila ducked into the hallway and bolted into the bathroom. "Oh, ye of little faith. Do you really think

I would let Elspeth come without having my own exit plan?"

Holly popped her head around the door and peered down the hallway, before jerking back and closing them inside the bathroom. "Whatever you have planned, execute it now. We've got Muses hot-footing it our way."

"Right." Lila shoved a large window open and leaned a little way out. "You ready?" Getting a murmured ascent, Lila drew back and waved her cousins over. "Climb out. I have an associate on the other side who'll help you down. Hurry up." Lila linked her hands together. "Put your foot here and I'll boost you up."

Shrugging, Xandie slid a foot into Lila's hands and yelped as Lila heaved her up to the window. Slim arms reached up and helped Xandie dismount on the other side. Lila wiped her hands on her jeans and then got back into position. "Right, banshee. Your turn."

Holly backed up. "You know what? I think I'm fine. I can distract the Muses so you guys escape."

Lila growled, imitating her hellhound. "Get here now."

"I hate my family." Giving in, Holly shifted

forward and gingerly placed a foot in Lila's hands. "This is safe, right?"

"As long as your booty doesn't get stuck, you'll be fine. Now jump."

"You know I hate my family, right?" Holly pushed herself up with Lila's boost and slid through the window, disappearing out of sight.

"You should share my drama llama nickname because I think you're a closet drama queen. Now stop whining." Lila braced against the sink and heaved herself up and through the open window. At least she tried to...until she snagged on the window latch. "Oh, come on." Lila banged on the building as she hung upside down.

"Whose booty is too big to get through the window now?" Holly crowed.

"Just get me out of here before we all get caught."

"Hang on." Xandie slid up next to Lila and gripped something on the window, pushing it out of the way. "Drag her out now."

"No, no dragging. Just gently prying," Lila wailed as Holly and Edie each grabbed an arm and pulled.

"Ouch." Lila shot forward and collapsed on top of her cousin. Muffled shrieks coming from under Lila's chest had her rolling to the side.

Holly's red face emerged, gasping for air. "Time to give up sweets, Lila, if you want a life of crime."

"You're just jealous you don't have these curves." Lila stood and shimmied in place.

"That was so much fun. You Harrows are hilarious." Edie bent over double, fighting laughter. "Just wish I'd seen Elspeth strut down the runway in her bra headwear."

"Wait until you see my encore out the front of the Academy." In front of them, still wearing her cone bra and holding her similarly decorated feline, stood a teenage Elspeth.

"Couldn't help yourself, could you?" Holly glared at her grandmother. "Just once would it kill you to act your age?"

Lila and Xandie inhaled noisily and stepped away from the Elspeth blast.

"Just once can't you find a date? Is it too much for this old grandmother to expect all her grandkids married with babies?" Elspeth glared right back, but the impact was lessened because of her underwear head covering.

"Could we get going? I'm pretty sure the Muse patrol is zeroing in on us as we speak." Lila tapped a foot, waiting for one of the warring Harrows to give.

"Fine." Holly growled and dropped her gaze.

"Don't think I won't forget the desperate and date-less comment."

"Ditto, soon to be regretful Banshee." Elspeth beamed and strolled off toward the front of the Academy.

"Are you crazy?" Xandie shook her head at Holly as they trailed behind their grandmother. "Since when do you stand up to Elspeth?"

Holly grimaced. "All the chaos lately, it's just doing my head in. Why can't Point Muse and the Harrows be calm and peaceful?"

Lila skidded to a stop near the front of the Academy where stone statues of the nine muses stood.

Grinning madly, Elspeth swung her arms above her head. "Ta-da." She twerked in celebration of her handiwork.

"Let Hades devour me whole, right now, in Tartarus." Holly blinked her eyes multiple times, but the image remained.

"This is why Harrows have a bad name in town." Lila rubbed her aching forehead. Elspeth had attached nine cone bras to the anatomically correct nine muses statues.

"It looks even better than I planned, plus those fussy pants have no clue who decorated the girls, because I'm in disguise. It's a brilliantly devious scheme." Elspeth clapped her hands.

"Not this time, Mother." Winifred strode up to Elspeth and uncorked a potion bottle. "Some days you just have to take your punishment and deal with the consequences. You'll never learn from your mistakes otherwise." Winifred flung some of the potion at Elspeth and then Colin.

"Winifred Claire Harrow, you'll pay for this." Elspeth's tracksuit and her blonde wig drooped as her features and body returned to normal.

"I'm sorry, Mom, but you need to learn the right time and place." Winifred crossed her arms as the three head mistresses gathered behind her.

A pink-haired muse, visibly shaking with rage, pointed a finger at Elspeth. "That was your last chance, Harrow."

"We will not allow you on Academy property anymore," the blue-headed muse chimed in.

"And we called law enforcement as what you've done constitutes desecration." The green-haired muse bellowed over a shoulder, "Officer Braun, we found her."

One of the Point Muse deputies, Caleb Braun, shuffled over to Elspeth, spelled handcuffs extended. "Now, Elspeth, let's get this over and done with. All easy, okay?" Brown hair flopped over Caleb's face and he shoved it back with a shaking hand.

Poor Caleb looked terrified. The normally energetic and muscled bear shifter always had his twin brother, Riley, in tow. Both brothers shared pale blue eyes, brown hair and broad bear shifter shoulders, but this time Caleb was alone. Not even his older brother, Zach, was in attendance.

"Never show weakness to a predator." Melody Braun, another deputy, and the Braun's younger sister, popped up next to Lila. "I warned him not to, but those Muses can be persuasive."

"Couldn't Aggie have stopped him?" Holly nudged Melody. "I mean, he's gonna pay for this for a very long time. Elspeth never forgets."

"Ma went for her annual back waxing. Caleb manned the switch and copped the Muses. He crumbled."

"What about Zach? Surely he could have talked the Muses down?" Xandie frowned, searching the area for her chief of police boyfriend.

Melody shot Edie an uncomfortable look. "I shouldn't mention anything."

Lila glared at her noncommittal friend. "Spit it out, bear."

"Fine," Melody groaned and lowered her voice.

"Zach got a tip-off and then received a report Winchester House had been broken into. Riley and that reaper as well as Zach headed out to investigate."

"And?" Lila prodded friend. "That can't be all you've got. That's a pitiful amount of gossip."

"He and Riley are executing a search warrant for evidence relating to the murders in connection to Edie Winchester. The tip-off was very detailed."

"What?" Edie backed up, waving her hand. "There is no evidence. I haven't hurt anyone, I swear."

Lila grabbed Xandie and Holly. "Get Edie to the Library. Braun can't arrest her if he can't find her."

"The first place he'll look is the bakery or Harrow House. Then the Library. You won't be able to run from him." Melody winced. "He'll be on your trail soon enough."

"Nope, Xandie can talk to her precious Library about hiding Edie." Lila winked at her cousin.

Sighing, Xandie grabbed hold of the shaking Edie and guided her toward Lila's bakery van. "I can see couples' counselling in my future."

"At least you qualify for couples' counselling, that's more than we have." Lila indicated her and Holly.

Truth be told, it was hard to date in a town where everyone knew your business. Lila tore her mind away from her lack of dating back to the problem at hand...

Hiding Edie from Point Muse law enforcement.

SIXTEEN

"Stalkers will be prosecuted."

Lila squealed, hand over her racing heart, as Matthew Grim leaned over her. "Dude, seriously, make some noise next time. You'll give someone a heart attack one of these days."

"Like the one Braun's going to have when he sees you lurking."

Lila stood and dusted her jeans. "I have no clue what you're talking about. I'm standing on the pavement, which is a public thoroughfare."

"You're crouched down, peering through gaps in a fence. Pretty sure that's classified as lurking."

"If that sneaky bear shifter would share information, then I wouldn't have to lurk." Lila pinned her annoying reaper with a stern glare. "Now give. Why is Braun at Winchester House?"

Grim leaned against the fence that bordered Winchester House property. "He received an anonymous tip that the Winchesters were hiding evidence, plus a report of a break-in at the House."

Lila stepped back and gave Winchester House the once over. "Anonymous. Yeah, right. This has Chloe Sylvis' manicured paws all over it."

"Whoever called it in, Zach needed to investigate."

"Has he found anything yet?" The last thing Edie needed was more fuel tossed on the suspect fire. The bunny shifter played a dangerous game and if she wasn't careful, an innocent woman would go to jail.

"I'm not sure. I'm out here dealing with stalkers." Grim winked.

She really needed to get inside Winchester House. Preferably, without the ever-vigilant police chief spotting her. Lila focused on Matthew and smiled slowly.

The reaper took a step back. "When you smile like that, I feel like I'm on the menu for dinner."

Lila widened her smile and trailed a hand over Matthew's chest. Hard muscles and a fiery warmth seared her palm. Coughing, Lila dropped her hand, but still fluttered her eyelashes. "Why, dear Matthew, what a funny thing to say."

"Got something in your eye?"

"Oh, for Hecate's sake. There's nothing in my eye." Lila scowled. So much for her flirting skills. "Get me inside Winchester House, reaper, and you'll have unlimited access to my baked goods and can even organize my office however you want. Deal?"

"Were you flirting?" Matthew's voice pitched high on the last word, and he coughed to clear his throat. "If those are your terms, I accept." His voice dropped lower and he crowded Lila as he stepped forward. "Stay close, Lila Marie Harrow. It'd be a pity for Braun to arrest you for interfering in his investigation." His body brushed against Lila's as he shifted past.

She gulped down excess drool and focused on the reaper's back as he led the way toward the back garden of Winchester House. "Why are we here? I need to get into the House, not take time to sniff the roses."

"Oh, doubting Harrow." Matthew directed Lila toward a walled garden of herbs. "Use your power of observation and check out the potting shed."

Lila peered around the gate at the crime scene

brownies, Braun and Riley, his youngest brother and deputy. "Why are they out here? We already know they found the Ipecac plant in the garden."

"Watch." Grim settled behind Lila, his chest pressed against her back.

Braun's younger brother carried two small wooden crates out of the potting shed. From where she stood, Lila heard the clink of glass. "Potion bottles?"

"I think so from the look of it."

"He's going to blame Edie for this. What's the bet those bottles contain traces of venom, in particular Lamia venom."

"No takers here. But that isn't all." Matthew took his phone out and showed Lila a photo he'd taken earlier. "He also found this."

Lila squinted at the photo. "That ripped paper? How does that implicate Edie?"

Matthew enlarged the photo and showed it to Lila again. "Does that help?"

She hissed as she recognized it. "They're pages torn out of Rufus' ledger."

"And they mention E. Winchester selling Rufus venom. Braun thinks she sold Lamia venom to Moon before he died."

"Nope." Lila shook her head. "No way Edie

could be a Lamia, if that's what you're implying."

"Then how did the pages become hidden in her room, under a floorboard?"

"Someone wants to make sure she's arrested." Lila pushed Grim away. "I need to get back to Edie. Make sure Braun can't find her until we track down the real killer, or at least another viable suspect that gets his interest off her."

"Is it pointless to ask you to stay out of trouble?"

"Trouble is a Harrow's middle name." Lila blew the reaper a kiss and hurried off. The evidence piled up against Edie. Lila knew Braun would hunt her down first thing.

Time wasn't on Edie's side.

"We've got issues." Lila burst into the Library and slammed the door shut.

"When don't Harrows have issues?" Holly shrugged.

Nash padded over to Lila and nuzzled her leg. "Hey, buddy." Lila reached down and gave Nash a quick rub. "Not Harrow issues. Edie issues."

"What now?" Edie moaned, pacing in front of the large bay windows that faced the sea.

"Braun received an anonymous tip-off about evidence at Winchester House, along with a break-in report." Lila collapsed onto the chair next to Xandie's desk.

"Did he tell you about the tip-off?"

Lila stared at her cousin. "Your boyfriend snuck off to Winchester House without saying a word. Grim told me."

"Why go to Winchester House? I didn't hurt anyone. What kind of evidence could they find?"

"Potion bottles in the potting shed. The most damaging piece of evidence were pages from the ledger that mention E. Winchester selling venom to Rufus. The same pages that were accidentally torn from the ledger when the Lamia sprayed the venom in my eyes."

"Whoever the Lamia is, they're trying to frame Edie." Xandie jumped up and joined Edie in pacing.

"Correct, and your love bear will be here any moment to take Edie in. I can guarantee it."

Holly sat up and pointed at Xandie. "Time to take a stand, cuz. Say no to boyfriends arresting innocent women. Solidarity, sista," Holly whooped but cut off the noise when everyone stared at her. "Just trying to keep the vibe upbeat."

"Don't. Just don't." Xandie sighed, and then

placed a hand on the wall. "Library? Could we go to incognito mode, please? We don't want Zach arresting Edie." The lights in the Library dimmed and an echoing click from both internal and external doors sounded throughout the room. The glass in the bay windows darkened until the view of the ocean became slightly obscured.

"Thanks, Library." Xandie blew a kiss into the air. "No one can get in or see in from the outside. That should keep Zach at bay until we find evidence to clear Edie."

"If we can find any," Holly muttered. "Look, we all know Edie didn't commit murder, but the Lamia is covering her snake tracks pretty well."

"Aha." Xandie clicked fingers. "I've got more information that might help." She opened a drawer in a desk and grabbed a handful of handwritten pages. "I wrote some notes. Basically, even though there's little information on the Lamia in the Library, I did find something interesting on snake shifters."

"Details?"

"It's about the Sylvis family. I did a deep dive into their family history and found a snake connection. Somewhere along the line, way back when, a bunny shifter mated with a snake shifter. There's been documented instances of snake shifting gifts cropping up in the family linage. It's rare and there hasn't been one noted for a generation, but it's still recorded in their family history."

"Kinda makes Chloe Sylvis a more likely suspect. Doesn't it?" Lila mused.

Holly frowned. "Does that make Chloe our Lamia?"

"It certainly gives Edie some reasonable doubt. And that's all we need." Xandie jerked as a heavy pounding on the Library's internal door sounded out of the blue.

"Give it up, Harrows. I know you have Edie hidden in there. You aren't doing her any favors by keeping her away from me." Zach Braun's irritated bear tones flowed through the heavy wooden door.

Everyone froze.

"Xandie. Theo's already told me you're all holed up in there, plotting. You might as well let me in."

"Traitor," Xandie hissed at the conspicuously absent black cat.

Lila jumped up. "Holly and I will go follow Chloe, see what turns up. You keep an eye on Edie."

Xandie shook her head. "If I know Zach, he has one of his brothers watching the house in case you sneak out, and Zach won't leave until I talk to him. He's a stubborn bear." Xandie glanced around the room. "Library? Open the anteroom, make sure no one can enter the room except for Lila and myself." She opened the door to a small waiting room that had another door leading outside. "Edie, you can wait here until I get rid of Braun."

Edie slipped into the room with a smile of thanks.

"Now I can go and distract Zach with this Chloe snake shifter information while you, Holly and Nash sneak out the back."

Holly stood with a sigh. "All this rushing around is exhausting, plus how do we escape Zach's brother who's watching the house. Wouldn't Lila's van parked out the front be a dead giveaway?"

"Nope. I parked down the road and I walked up in case we needed a secret getaway."

"And the front isn't the only way to escape." Xandie pointed to the sea and her private beach below. "The Merrows are always sunning themselves at my dock. Get them to take you to the harbor. Zach will never expect escape by sea. It's a perfect plan."

"Except for the fact we have to get wet. Do you have any idea how long my hair takes to dry?" Holly groaned.

"Good hair just don't care. Now mush, shiny witch. We have a mermaid to catch." Lila dragged

Holly to the back door. Nash already waited at the exit. The cousins stopped just outside, hugging the wall until they got the signal to go.

Xandie paused until they were out of sight, before flinging the door open to confront her boyfriend. "What's got your bear shifter bone so grumpy? Someone stole your porridge?"

Zach burst into the room, with Theo, Xandie's black cat, with him. "That crack about Goldilocks isn't funny. Her rap sheet is a mile long. Where are Edie and Lila?"

Xandie shrugged. "I currently have no clue where Lila is. She's a Harrow, who knows what goes on in her head? Besides, I'd be more concerned about Caleb arresting Elspeth for underwear desecration of the Muses statues at the Academy."

"He what?" Braun froze like a deer in headlights. "Tell me he didn't."

Xandie smiled widely. "Oh, he did. Aggie had already left for her back wax and you must've been out of the office. I watched him arrest Elspeth with spelled cuffs."

"You Harrows will send me into early retirement."

Taking pity on her poor beleaguered boyfriend, Xandie brushed a kiss against his cheek. "Never mind, sweetie. I'm sure Elspeth won't blame you. *Much.*" She led Braun to the couch and settled him down. "I do have some research I think you need to see." Xandie waved a hand behind her back at Lila and Edie.

Taking her cousin's lead, Lila stopped eavesdropping and scooted out into the formal gardens. Making sure Holly followed, Lila skirted the stone statues in the middle of the garden and headed for the stairs that lead down from Xandie's bluff to the beach and the dock below.

"If we're in luck, one of the girls can give us a lift into town." Lila pointed to the Merrows, in particular one woman in a rhinestone-studded bra top with an iridescent purple fishtail.

Nash panted and joyfully bounded up to the Merrow, liberally covering the giggling woman's face in sloppy kisses.

"Have I mentioned I dislike swimming intensely?" Holly grouched.

"You'd hate being arrested for interfering in a police investigation even more." Lila shoved her cousin at the Merrow.

Lila knew in her bones that Chloe Sylvis had something to do with the murders. *All she had to do was prove it...*

SEVENTEEN

"Don't do it. Just don't do it." Lila backed away from her grinning hellhound.

Nash ignored Lila and shook his head. Seawater drenched Lila and Holly.

Holly glared at her cousin. "*Let's go down the beach, the Merrows can give us a lift into town, it will be fine.* Now it looks like I swam the whole way."

"Hey. We're lucky that they had a little boat available for us to use. We might have had to swim the whole way." Lila held up her hands. "Calm down. I didn't say all of that anyway. Xandie did. But she did get us out from under Braun's nose. Besides, the Merrows did us a favor and you didn't have to swim."

"*We* didn't, but your dog did. He's a hellhound. Surely he hates water and likes fire?"

"I have no clue. I blame Hades for everything." Lila shrugged.

Nash whined, looking guilty. He reared back and breathed gently on the women. Warm flowing air covered the cousins and dried clothing and hair.

"Who's a good hairdryer?" Lila smothered Nash's heads in kisses before straightening. "See? Nash had it handled."

"Your puppy covered me in doggy breath. How is that any better?" Holly glared at Lila.

"Stop complaining, we've got murders to solve." Lila looked up and down the dock. The Merrows had dropped them off at the harbor at the bottom of town. Thankfully, in the opposite direction from the Library. Hopefully, they could avoid Braun's sticky paws long enough to clear Edie's name.

"Right, I need to check on the bakery, then scout around. If you spot Chloe or anything that looks suspicious, call me. You stay around downtown and keep an eye out." Lila eyed the sky. "Won't be too long and it'll be dark. We need to wrap this up. Now scoot."

"Yeah, yeah." Holly waved to Lila and ambled toward the park at the end of the harbor.

"Come on, Nash. Let's go check on the bakery. Then find a murderer." Lila faked a casual stroll and headed toward Main Street.

"Psss. Lila. Over here." A familiar voice hailed Lila in a loud whisper.

Couldn't escape the Harrow family, no matter where in Point Muse you were. Lila headed over to her aunt's potion and candle store. "What's up, Aunt Winifred?"

"Quickly." Winifred shot an arm out and dragged Lila into her shop. She turned the open sign to closed and locked the door.

"Well, that's all cloak and dagger."

Nash slipped up next to Winifred, begging for cuddles. Lila's aunt gave him a quick cuddle and kiss before she turned back to Lila.

"Xandie let us know you're on the loose and hiding from the police. I thought discretion might be a good idea."

"You make Holly and me sound like escaped criminals."

"It's probably in your future."

"Thanks for the vote of confidence, Aunt Win."

"I *am* a Harrow." Winifred shrugged. "I saw that mouthy bunny and her daughter arguing earlier."

What a surprise. "I think Chloe argues with everyone."

Winifred pursed her lips. "Not like this. Her daughter seemed worried. Told her to stop or she'd end up like the others. Chloe told her not to worry, it would all be over soon enough and then she patted her bag."

Like that didn't sound ominous at all. "Did she say anything else?"

"Not to her daughter, the kid stormed off after that. But she rang someone as soon as her daughter left."

"Any idea who?"

"No clue, but it wasn't a friendly call. The mean bunny taunted them with something that she'd taken. Told them if they wanted it back, they had to pay the price."

What did Chloe have that someone would want badly enough for her to blackmail them?

"After that, she hung up and cackled to herself and headed toward your bakery."

Curious and curiouser. Point Muse and its residents, always an enigma wrapped up in a puzzle. "Thanks, Aunt Win. If you see the others, I'm heading to my bakery and Holly's lurking around town somewhere."

"Will do." Aunt Winifred enveloped Lila in a hug. "You're doing great at sleuthing. Just don't forget you always have backup."

Nash whined and pawed at the door, eager to be outside.

"How can I forget?" Lila opened the door and checked up and down the street before she sauntered out.

"I think Chloe has taken up Brittany's idea of blackmail. We just have to find out who," Lila told Nash.

The hellhound stiffened and pulled off to the side of the pavement, hugging the side of the building.

"What's up, pup?" Hades' fierce tracker had caught the scent of prey for sure. But what prey?

"Bunny." Nash kept his head to the ground, intent on the trail.

Speak of the bunny, and she shall hop right into view. Lila watched as Chloe strutted across the road near the bakery, something bound in plastic clasped to her chest.

Lila ducked into a shop doorway. Nash crowded in next to her as the shifter glanced up and down the road before darting into the alley next to Lila's shop.

"Well, well, well. What's the little bunny up to?"

Before Lila could bust the bunny, another figure scuttled across the road, meeting Chloe at the mouth of the alley as she came back out.

"Hecate's lost marbles, Edie. What are you doing out in public?" Lila cursed. Harrow's bad luck strikes again. *The clueless bear shifter would come lumbering in and arrest Edie any second now.* Lila silently mimed a scream before focusing back on the warring duo, who had resorted to shoving each other. "Next thing there will be pulling of hair and we'll have a real witch versus bunny fight." Breaking skulking cover, Lila stepped out of the shadow of the store, just as a white van drew alongside the squabbling women.

The door slid open and a masked figure jumped out, white cloth in hand.

Chloe and Edie stopped arguing as the figure bolted toward them and shoved the cloth over Chloe's face. The bunny shifter struggled for a few minutes before sagging. Then the kidnapper lugged Chloe into the van and turned back to Edie.

Lila roared a warning and bolted toward their friend. She was too late. The kidnapper dragged a shocked Edie inside the van as well. The door slammed shut and the van roared off, careening around the corner and out of sight.

"Burnt Brownies," Lila cursed and ran to her bakery. She had to call Braun. Let him know someone else had Chloe and Edie.

Someone completely not on her list of one suspect.

Someone not Chloe Sylvis had just entered the picture.

Hester popped her head out of the bakery door just as Lila ran up. "What's the ruckus? We were just about to close."

Lila bent over, panting. "Someone in a white van just kidnapped Chloe and Edie. Call Braun."

Hester popped back inside, then Lila heard raised voices. Grim charged out, checking Lila over from head to foot.

She waved him off. "I'm fine. I wasn't close enough to get hurt." As Lila spoke, Nash lowered his head to the ground and wandered around, before disappearing into the alley.

"Can you tell me what happened?"

Focusing her attention back on the reaper, Lila gave him a synopsis. "We hid Edie at the Library. Then Holly and I snuck out to look for Chloe. I found Edie and Chloe arguing. Next thing I know, a white van rolls up and a masked person jumps out. Puts a white cloth over Chloe's mouth and packs both Chloe and Edie in the van and roars off."

Lila trailed off, thinking hard. Winifred said Chloe had blackmailed someone over the phone. Then Lila saw Chloe carrying something into the alley. The same alley that Nash just disappeared into. The kidnapper and the person talking to Chloe were probably one and the same. They'd kidnapped the shifter to get back what the bunny had stolen. Maybe Chloe had hidden whatever it was in the alley?

"Lila? Lila, what's wrong?" Grim tapped Lila on the head. "Earth to Baker?"

Lila shook his hand off and followed Nash's into the alley. She found him near the dumpster, sniffing around the base. "What did you find?"

"Bunny stink." Nash pawed at the dumpster.

Lila sighed. *What one does to solve a crime.* "Dumpster diving it is." She grabbed the lid of the dumpster and flung it off with a metallic clang.

"Tell me you aren't going through your own garbage?" Matthew grimaced and took a step away. "When was that thing last emptied?"

"A while ago. Pickup's tomorrow, so I need to check it now." Lila shoved a wooden crate up to the dumpster and balanced on top.

"Whoa, Lila. Wait." The reaper grabbed the

back of Lila's shirt before she threw herself in. "You don't know what's in there."

Lila peered down. "Garbage, that's what. Now let me go or get in there yourself."

Matthew dropped Lila's shirt. "The things I do for you." He carefully lifted Lila off the crate. "Here, hold this." He handed her his pen-sized scythe before heaving himself over the side. He balanced on the trash and cocked an eyebrow at Lila. "Just what am I looking for?"

The reaper was her hero in the dumpster. Butterflies flip-flopped at the base of Lila's stomach. She cleared her throat and ignored the silly fluttering in the stomach. "I have no clue, but I think it's square and covered in plastic. She didn't have much time to hide it before they kidnapped her."

"It's likely to be near the top." Matthew crouched down and sorted through the piles of trash.

Lila shoved Matthew's scythe into her pocket, stepped onto the crate and peered over, wrinkling her nose. "That's nasty. Like a combination of Colin's radioactive stench, Nash's hellhound breath and Elspeth's failed potion experiments."

"Try standing in it." Matthew used a broken broom to poke through rotting piles of trash.

"Anything?"

"Nothing. Except for the fact you need to recycle more."

"Yeah, yeah, everyone's an expert. Hey." Lila pointed to the far corner of the dumpster. "What's that?"

Matthew shifted closer and used his broom to uncover a plastic-wrapped object.

"That's it." Lila whooped and wobbled on the crate. She balanced a hand on the edge of the dumpster.

"Catch." Matthew grabbed the plastic object and pretended to throw it at Lila.

She leaned forward, hand outstretched, trying to grab the square parcel. "Stop fooling around and give it to me."

Matthew smirked. "How about you come in here and get it?"

Smart-mouthed reaper. Steeling herself, Lila clambered over the edge. "Fine. I'm in here. Now give it."

The reaper gaped at Lila. "I didn't actually think you'd get in."

"If I want something, I get my hands dirty. Now gimme." Lila took a step forward. Trash bags and slimy food waste shifted under her feet. Her arms wind-milled as the bag beneath her caved in. "No," Lila wailed as she flew forward.

Matthew dropped Chloe's hidden load and grabbed for Lila, dragging both of them down flat on top of the trash. He cradled her and flicked a squished half-eaten cupcake off her forehead, leaving a blue smear behind.

"Whoops." Lila tried to take a breath but changed it to a cough as rotting fruit smell wafted over her. "I think I have something smeared on my behind. Feels like it's soaking in."

Matthew shook with laughter. "I have no clue what I'm sitting on, but everywhere I move, it squeaks. Is this the Harrow luck I keep hearing about?"

Lila stared up into Matthew's gleaming gray eyes. "Might be my luck. The Harrow ones normally involve bodies and Colin's upset stomach."

"I think the dumpster smell might rival even his stench." He trailed a finger down Lila's cheek.

"You might be right." Her voice squeaked as the reaper drew closer, his breath sweet and minty compared to the rot around them. His lips ghosted along her cheek and claimed her mouth. Electricity sparked the butterflies into a frenzy dance party.

"Is this a normal make-out place? I never thought

a dumpster was an overly romantic place, especially after witnessing a kidnapping."

Zach Braun's frosty tones froze Lila. She opened her eyes, staring into Matthew's twinkling ones.

"Now I'm the one with bad luck." He smirked and moved Lila away from him. He leaned around and grabbed Chloe's parcel.

"Your plastic-wrapped clue, Sherlock Baker."

Lila swallowed around a dry throat and fought the blush that flared as she grabbed the small package. "Thanks," she said in a small voice.

Braun reached in an arm and snagged Lila's shirt. "Let me help you there, Lila Marie Harrow. I'd hate for you to slip and disappear."

Oh, poor little bear shifter was definitely miffed. Lila used his boost and clambered out, Matthew following.

The chief of police glared at Lila. "Can you tell me why you hid Edie and why she and Chloe Sylvis have apparently been kidnapped?"

Lila brushed unmentionable food detritus off her jeans. "Edie's innocent and they're both been kidnapped because of this." She held up a package.

Braun crossed his arms. "And what is this?"

She knew exactly what Chloe's package was.

"Rufus Moon's ledger. Someone knew she'd stolen it. That's the reason for the kidnapping."

For the first time in this entire investigation, Lila finally felt one step ahead.

And now she had leverage...

EIGHTEEN

"Why does the war room always end up in the bakery?" Lila dumped a plate of iced cakes on the table.

"Because you have free food?" Holly grabbed a brightly frosted cake and took a large bite. She mumbled something as she chewed.

"Pardon?" Lila grimaced. "I can't hear through your gluttony."

Holly swallowed her mouthful before speaking. "Set the table and they will come."

"Pearls of wisdom. How about we focus on how we plan to get Edie back?" Lila crossed her arms and glowered at the room.

"And Chloe, too. Right?" Xandie arched one eyebrow. "It's not just Edie we're looking for."

Lila waved a hand around. "Yeah, yeah, Chloe, too."

The door to the bakery flew open. Braun and Grim stood silhouetted in the doorway. The bear shifter closed the door behind them and lowered his head to brush a kiss across Xandie's cheek.

"Don't suppose you have honey cakes?" he asked in a hopeful tone.

"Sorry, sweetie. You're cut off until the op is over. You're too much of a liability when on the hard stuff." Xandie patted Zach's whiskered face.

"Harsh, Harrow. Harsh. "

Grim ignored the honey cake argument. "I guess you have a plan?"

"I have an idea. I still need to get a few supplies though."

Braun finished squabbling with Xandie. "You saw Chloe and Edie kidnapped, Lila. Who do you think's behind it?"

"Not Chloe." Lila grimaced. "Thought for sure the maniacal bunny was our baddie, especially since snake shifting runs through the Sylvis family. But considering she and Edie were kidnapped, I figure that clears them both."

Fixing Lila with a piercing stare, Braun nodded. "And?"

"And what?"

"You're a Harrow. Your family always has a backup plan and a backup suspect. So, who's the Lamia?"

Everyone in the bakery held their breath as Lila opened and closed her mouth a few times before answering. "I'm pretty sure I know who it is, but I've been wrong once already. So, no names until I can stare them in their snaky face."

"Spoilsport," Grim whispered in Lila's ear.

She took a sidestep and pointed an accusing finger at him. "No flirting the answer out of me either."

"Me?" Grim pointed to himself and let loose a low chuckle.

Turning her back on the way-too-happy reaper, Lila concentrated on remembering details of the kidnapping. "The masked person who jumped out seemed stocky and strong. But I don't think they were young. They were stiffer, not as flexible as a younger person."

Braun nodded. "And the driver?"

"Didn't move out of the driver's seat, so I barely saw them. Both had masks on and something covering their heads. But I'm pretty sure Edie recognized them and that's why they took her as well. She seemed almost too shocked to move, that's why they nabbed her so easily."

"And the goal for the kidnapping is that thing?" Xandie pointed to the ledger that sat on the table.

"Yup. I've gone through Rufus' records and it lays out names, dates, Lamia and snake venom. I have a pretty good timeline for everything. *And* everyone involved now. "

Braun paced the floor. "It will be an exchange, ledger for the girls. We'll have to set up a drop, and surveillance. Nab them when they produce their leverage."

Elspeth slammed the kitchen door open, standing panting in the bakery.

Colin scooted in between her legs and rolled over onto his back, legs in the air. "My pugley body is not built for speed."

"Neither is Elspeth." Holly winked at Lila.

"Enough, smart mouth. I bring kidnapper tidings." Elspeth paused dramatically, making sure every eye trained on her. "The kidnapper's contacted the Sylvis family. Straight swap. Chloe for the ledger."

"And Edie?"

Elspeth shook her head at Lila's question. "No mention of Edie at all."

Interesting... "Time and place for swap?"

"Ten tonight at the picnic tables near the funeral home. Only one representative allowed."

Braun rubbed his hands. "I'll get a team in place. After they give me Chloe and Edie, I'll signal for them to move in and take the kidnappers."

"Nope." Elspeth pointed at Lila. "They only want our little baker. No one else."

Grim growled. "No way. Lila's a baker, not a hostage negotiator. She's not qualified."

Colin rolled over and sniffed the ground for stray crumbs. "She's a Harrow. If anything, she's overqualified. Besides, my dame will be watching. She's the best backup a girl could have."

Elspeth cackled and this time the lights stayed bright.

"Losing your touch, Elspeth." Lila pointed to the light fixtures overhead.

"Conserving my power reserves for tonight. Who knows what might happen with a Lamia on the loose? I can just feel the dark energy churning."

"Right, Lamia. Hostage exchange." Lila swallowed the lump that magically appeared at the back of her throat.

Grim stood next to Lila and leaned in, lowering

his voice a little. "You don't need to do this, no matter what the kidnappers say."

Time to Harrow up, drama llama. She gave herself a mental pep talk. Xandie had placed herself in danger too many times to count and she always had Harrow backup and made it out alive. So would she. Lila took a deep breath and nodded to Matthew. "I'm good. I have a plan and you guys will be blending with the shadows nearby. I've got this."

Holly scooted over to wrap Lila tight in a bear hug. "You're so brave... Can I have your apartment if anything happens? Living in Harrow House is wearing my nerves down."

Lila pried Holly's arms from around her. "Yes, sweet optimistic cousin. If I happen to come off second best to a murderous Lamia and need to visit Hades, you get my apartment."

"Woot." Holly wiggled in a circle, performing her own version of a victory dance. Everyone stared open-mouthed at her. "What? It's best to get these things locked down in front of witnesses. That way there's no confusion or fighting over assets after someone passes. Working at the funeral home taught me that."

"This family never fails to surprise." Braun rubbed his forehead. "Can we please get back to our game plan? We only have a few hours to get every-thing in place now."

"It's simple. I'm at the picnic table, Nash can come with me. Xandie and Holly take point at the funeral home. Braun and Grim wait nearby with backup, ready to bust the Lamia."

Elspeth crossed arms and tapped a foot. "And me, dear granddaughter? Where will I be?"

Lila smiled wide, teeth bared. "You, wicked witch of Point Muse, will be lurking in the shadows, ready to pounce and suck the life energy out of the evil doers if they get out of line. How does that sound?"

"I am a tad peckish." Elspeth giggled and skipped around the table before coming to a halt in front of Lila. All humor drained away and she patted her granddaughter on the cheek. "We got this, little baker. You can count on family."

"I'm feeling all sorts of weird familial affection, it's discombobulating." Lila stepped back from Elspeth. "Can we go back to sarcastic jabs at each other? It's my comfort zone."

Lila's grandmother winked. "I need to get the right outfit together, anyway. Tootles." She gathered Colin up and wandered out, muttering about color coordination.

"On that note, scoot, everyone. I have a few supplies to source." Lila rubbed her hands, a plan unfolding in her head.

"Are you going to let us in on your devious scheme?" Xandie, who had remained relatively quiet during the planning, finally spoke up.

"Nope. I do have an idea of what I want to do, but I'm just basically going to wing it."

And hope for the best.

"Is it just me, or does it feel like the zombie apocalypse is imminent... *Again?*"

Nash huffed at Lila's comment and settled himself into the shadows under the picnic table.

Lila rubbed her arms and shivered. She had no clue if nerves or the cold affected her but standing in the dark, next to a funeral home, about to meet a fanged killer, didn't feel comfortable.

The classical Greek architecture of the Elysian Fields Funeral Home loomed behind her, the area dimly lit by old-fashioned lamp posts. The shadows seemed to have multiplied since Lila's arrival.

Whining softly, Nash gathered himself as dry rustling noises filled the suddenly silent park.

"Showtime, buddy. Hush now and let's wait for our trap to spring." Lila placed the ledger on the picnic table in plain view.

A few moments later the rustling noises stopped, and a balaclava-masked figure stepped into the weak light, dragging a bound and gagged Chloe Sylvis.

Lila fought an inappropriate snicker at the sight of the normally immaculately dressed bunny. Chloe's hair stood puffed out around her head in an over-teased bouffant beehive. Dirt smeared her face and clothing. "I like this new look on you, Chloe, makes you more approachable."

Chloe growled and shook bound hands at Lila.

The kidnapper dragged Chloe to the center of the small park only a half dozen paces away from the picnic table. "Ledger and you can have her."

The kidnapper had attempted to disguise their voice, but Lila, for once, knew exactly who she dealt with. She tapped the ledger. "As much as I'd love to take a homeless bunny off your hands, you have a friend of mine. No swaps until Edie's released."

The figure holding Chloe stiffened and looked over at one particularly dark shadow for direction.

The sound of rustling increased, along with a sibilant hissing.

Lila raised the voice. "You might as well come

out of the shadows. I know exactly who and what you are, and we aren't trading until I have Edie safe with me."

The Lamia hissed again and the kidnapper holding Chloe ripped off the balaclava, revealing Mildred's dour face. Another hiss and Mildred dropped Chloe to the ground and backed away. No wonder Emmaline Winchester appeared cold-blooded to everyone who met her. Being a Lamia made her part reptile. But she could still be provoked and when someone got angry, they made mistakes.

All Lila needed was one tiny little mistake...

"Are you a coward, Emmaline? Or just afraid to finally come out of the shadows and let Point Muse see you for what you really are?"

The dark shadows in the corner of the park shook violently and hissing echoed around the small area. Little green and yellow snakes shot out from the shadows, writhing in a reptilian ball toward Lila.

Mildred rushed back, dragging a similarly bound and gagged Edie. The housekeeper threw the youngest Winchester on the ground next to the bunny shifter.

"No swap until I see the glorious snake that is Emmaline Winchester. Come on, old girl, be loud and proud of your snakyness."

"Your mouth will get you killed, Lila Harrow."

Emmaline Winchester slid forward into the light, swaying.

Lila suppressed the shudder that gripped her entire body. The upper half of the old woman looked human. Long, stringy, reddish-gray hair fell over sagging skin, but her lower half gleamed with iridescent gold and green scales. The elderly woman rested on her large tail and swayed back and forth, hypnotically. Every so often, Lila saw a snake's forked tongue flicker out of the woman's mouth.

"This was the Winchesters' trouble, their dark secret, wasn't it? You're the Lamia."

"First prize."

Although slightly muffled, Emmaline's voice sounded remarkably human. Now to make her angry enough to make a mistake. "You used your own venom to make money? Isn't that kind of like selling yourself?"

Emmaline reared back. An opera of hisses accompanied her movement and the ball of small snakes rolled closer to Lila, forcing her up against the picnic table.

Nash growled softly from underneath the table. *Not yet, buddy.* Lila silently pleaded to the various gods above for Nash to remain still until the right time.

"Why shouldn't I profit from my curse? Others have used and hidden me away for decades for their own use."

"Your parents."

The Lamia's tail thrashed at the mention of her parents. "My family was ashamed of me. They kept me at home so they could control me. Unlike my sister, their favorite child."

"They moved Eudalia out of your reach, in case you snapped and ate her." Lila kept Emmaline talking. She needed the elderly snake woman distracted for her plan to work. Shadowed bushes behind the Lamia moved slightly and a small pug's tail stuck out for a moment before disappearing. Elspeth and Colin were in place and ready. Lila just had to do her part.

"I didn't hate her. I hated my parents. I wanted to escape Winchester House and Point Muse. That's all."

"You eloped with that Cygnus guy, Donald."

Emmaline moaned low in her throat. "He was a mistake. He said love would conquer all. Then I showed myself."

"I guess the green scales weren't quite what he expected to see on a honeymoon."

Swaying erratically now, Emmaline's chest shuddered, and her tongue flickered out every few seconds. "He swore he would still love me after I told him. No matter what, he would still be with me for eternity. But when he saw me, he ran. I couldn't stop myself. He'd become prey."

Eew, she'd eaten her husband. "I take it the boating accident was your cover story?"

"My parents. They hid me at Winchester House, hired Mildred to help me and then covered the sordid affair up. I became a recluse."

Lila pointed to the tail. "I guess you couldn't exactly roll around town like that."

"Decades ago, I could change at will. But the older I get, the ability to transform back to human gets weaker. I am permanently changed to a Lamia now."

"The wheelchair and the blanket." Lila clicked her fingers. "Smart thinking. But why snap now, kill Britney and Rufus, and frame Edie?"

Mildred inched forward, closer to Lila, who held a hand up. "No closer, evil hench woman or I disappear the ledger right into our Chief of Police's hands."

"You're a baker, not a witch. What could you do?" Mildred flexed a hand as she stared at the ledger on the picnic table.

"You'd be surprised what a little potion brewed by Elspeth Harrow will do." Lila unfolded the hand that tapped the ledger, showing the Lamia and her hench housekeeper the tiny little balloon. No need for them to know it was actually a cinnamon smoke bomb to disorient the snake woman and her reptilian minions.

"What do you want, Harrow?"

"An explanation. Why kill now?" Lila spotted Edie edging over to Chloe and tugging on her bound hands. Lila drew Mildred and Emmaline's attention to herself. "I mean, sure. You're stuck as half a snake. But why draw attention to yourself by killing someone?"

"Because that swan menace wanted money, she dug up the old rumor and put it all together. I had no choice. She would have brought the Winchester name into disrepute."

And murder didn't? Lila nodded thoughtfully.

"I knew she would bleed me dry of both Lamia venom and money. Then I saw her fighting with Moon. He had his ledger, and I knew that he wrote everything down. Every transaction. I no longer had a choice. They both had to go. It wasn't hard for Mildred and me to poison them. Who would suspect the upstanding Emmaline Winchester?"

"But Edie stayed at Winchester House. Sooner or later, she'd noticed something wasn't right."

Emmaline paused in her swaying with an unreadable expression on her face. "I have no ill will toward my great-niece. But I couldn't let her stop what I had started. I needed a way to remove her from the house."

Edie paused in her wrist untying and glared at her great-aunt.

"But what about Chloe? How did she get the ledger? You stole it from me after you spat venom in my eyes." Lila frowned at the Lamia. Waking up in hospital wasn't her fondest memory. She owed Emmaline for that.

"Sneaky bunny broke into my house and stole the ledger. Never trust furry shifters," the Lamia hissed in disgust. "Then she blackmailed me or tried to. Wanted me to step back from the Academy, give my venom to her." Emmaline jerked forward. "No one was using me again. It wasn't hard to plan her disappearance."

"And Edie was just collateral damage, plus she recognized Mildred. So, she had to disappear too."

"Yes," the Lamia hissed. "No one gets in my way, not even a Harrow." Emmaline whispered in a sibilant language to her snake minions. Unrolling, the yellow and green snakes undulated toward Lila.

Eyes aflame, Nash crawled out from the picnic table, let out an ear-piercing howl and lunged at the Lamia.

Mildred ran toward Nash, arms outstretched.

"I don't think so, hench woman." Lila raised a hand and pegged the balloon at Mildred. It burst and wreathed the housekeeper in cinnamon-scented smoke. Grabbing the ledger, Lila bolted forward, hollering. She raised the book and swung at Mildred, dropping the housekeeper like a stone to the ground.

As the smoke billowed toward her, the Lamia screeched and covered her face. She reared back from the sweetly scented haze.

"Ha." Lila patted herself on her shoulder in congrats and turned to the hostages. "Never underestimate a Harrow cinnamon smoke bomb. I knew researching how to repel reptiles with scent would come in handy someday."

"Never celebrate before a victory is won." Lila spun around to face the Lamia, who had now wrapped Nash in her coils. The hellhound's head canted to one side and his eyes spat flames, but he didn't seem overly upset. Maybe her pooch had a plan too. "Get your coils off my hound." Lila raised her voice. "Now would be a good time." The sound of pounding feet came from Lila's right side and Braun and Grim bolted into view, heading for the Lamia.

Xandie and Holly shot from behind the men and zeroed in on the unconscious Mildred. Both women leapt on top of the housekeeper, pinning her to the ground.

Leaving the men to untangle Nash, Lila dropped to the ground next to Edie and loosened her gag.

Edie took a deep breath and then exhaled. "I'm thinking of changing my name."

Lila giggled, concentrating on untying her hands. "You're not the first person in Point Muse who's said that."

Chloe grunted behind her gag, staring daggers at Lila. She held her hands up and waggled them.

Making sure Edie was okay, Lila turned to the bunny. "You brought this on yourself. If you hadn't tried to blackmail Emmaline, this wouldn't have happened."

Lila loosened the rope around Chloe's hands.

The bunny shifter yanked her gag away, taking shuddering breaths. "One does what one needs to for their family," she croaked out.

"Bet that's what Emmaline said too." Lila turned

and watched the Lamia as the men peeled the snake coils away from Nash. They threw themselves at the snake, but the snake tensed and slapped them with her tail.

Nash menaced the snake around the edges of the fight, blowing short spurts of flame at exposed scales when the men moved out of the way.

"Tally-ho, witches." Elspeth pounded in. Wearing a dark camo jogging suit, black stripes decorated across her face and a matching black skullcap, she raised an arm. She tossed a small black balloon at the Lamia and then one at Mildred.

Both Emmaline and Mildred froze. Unfortunately, so did Holly, who hadn't managed to clear the fallout zone before Elspeth launched.

Holly froze mid shriek at her grandmother.

Xandie skidded to a stop next to Lila. "I think Holly's the one that needs more cardio. Her reaction time's pitiful."

"Hold the snake," Elspeth directed the men. "I'm going to change her back to human. Maybe close your eyes. Her nude wrinkles might scare you young 'uns."

Xandie shrugged out of her jacket, holding it out toward the Lamia. "I'm ready. I'll protect your innocence, boys."

Lila rolled her eyes. "Since when are Point Muse residents, male or female, innocent?"

"Enough," Elspeth bellowed, then took a small packet from her inside her camo pants. She tipped a small amount of powder into her hand and blew gently. The powdery dust flew straight at Emmaline.

The Lamia, previously frozen, shivered. Her body convulsed and jerked. Grim and Braun grabbed the old woman as she sagged. Her snake bottom half dissolved into thin matchstick legs. Both men averted their gaze and Xandie ran up and wrapped the coat around the elderly woman.

Edie moved forward slowly, massaging her wrist. She waited for her great-aunt's eyes to open. When they did, she spoke, "I forgive you. What you went through as a young woman warped you, and what your parents did hurt even worse. Framing me was your protective mechanism snapping into place. But you can't hurt family. You stand together. The Harrows taught me that."

Emmaline coughed, sounding weak. "The Lamia genes skipped Eudalia. But you need to be ready if they surface in your children. Don't let them be treated like animals and locked away, ashamed of themselves."

Edie nodded, tears falling. "I won't. Snakes are

beautiful, graceful creatures, whether Lamia or full reptile. Everyone needs boundaries and good role models." Edie took a step back. "Goodbye, Great-Aunt Emmaline."

The old woman let out a small smile that twitched the corners of her mouth. "Goodbye, Edie."

Braun gently moved Emmaline toward a patrol car as his deputy brothers took Mildred into custody.

Elspeth pointed at Braun's deputy brother. "Don't think I've forgotten about the handcuff episode, Caleb Braun. You got your own reckoning coming."

"Wonder if she's planning on hexing his underwear drawer shut?" Matthew strolled up, Nash in his arms.

Lila's hellhound puppy sat quietly, snuggling with the reaper.

She had a sudden urge to evict her pup and place herself in the reaper's arms. Lila tried, but she couldn't banish the thought away. Time to take the reaper by the horns, instead of tiptoeing around the subject of them dating. Making a snap decision, Lila jutted her chin out and poked Grim on his chest. "Enough delaying tactics. You, me. A Harrow-free date. Take it or leave it. What do you say?"

Grim let out a deep belly laugh and handed

Nash over to Lila. His hands lingered on her arms as she settled Nash. "What do I say? It's about time, Harrow."

Lila blushed fiery red as the park erupted into cheers.

If a girl wanted something done right, she had to do it herself. Solving a murder *or* dating.

TWENTY

"Without me, those whippersnappers would've been Lamia snake food." Elspeth puffed out her non-existent chest and beamed at the room.

The last few days since Lila had rescued Chloe and Edie had been remarkably mayhem-free, so Lila and Matthew took the opportunity to sneak away for a picnic on Xandie's private beach. Except for the odd Merrow giggling and pointing, as first dates go, it'd scored a solid ten. They'd grabbed what private time they could, but now they were back with the rest of the family. Lila knew she should concentrate on whatever Elspeth was spouting, but she couldn't keep her mind off her time on the beach with Matthew.

"What are you thinking about that causes such red cheeks?"

The reaper's breath fanned Lila's skin and she leaned against him, his muscled warmth a tantalizing resting place. "None of your business, reaper. It might give you ideas."

"One can only hope," Grim murmured.

"Enough smooching," Elspeth hollered and then pointed at Xandie. "You, too, bookworm. We got some celebrating to do. Harrow style."

Xandie rolled her eyes. "In other words, stuff ourselves full of Lila's baking. Not exactly different to any other day around here."

"Except the Three Musketeers are down to one. One is the loneliest number," Holly intoned, and then spoiled the effect by poking out a cupcake-covered tongue.

"There's a reason you're single." Xandie turned to Lila. "Have you heard from Edie? Did she get home safely?"

"Yep, she's even spoken to Emmaline again. Her Great-Aunt has asked that she close the house up and sell it. Doesn't want to see it again. Eventually, if she and Mildred ever get out of the jailhouse, they're going to settle somewhere else together. So Edie will be back in a while."

"That's good. Helps her move on and deal with everything." Holly nodded sagely.

Lila snorted at Holly's wisdom, but she wasn't far wrong. She considered her cousin for a moment. Holly seemed off the last few murders. More whiny than humorous and sarcastic. Maybe the chaos and the mayhem the Harrows caused *was* finally whittling away at the banshee's last nerve. Holly needed a holiday.

The door to the bakery slammed open and Winifred jogged in, one hand to her chest as she fought for breath. She pointed over a shoulder as she gasped for air.

"For God's sake, daughter, spit out whatever's got your knickers in a twist." Elspeth grabbed one of the bear shifter's honey buns and took a large bite.

"A new shop's opening up across the road."

Lila shrugged. "Good. More shops in town, more people shopping, more money spent."

"You don't understand. It's a dessert bakery."

"What?" Lila shrieked and accidentally shoved an elbow in the reaper's ribs as she rushed to the window. "Delilah's Devilish Deserts. What kind of name is that?"

Elspeth spat out her mouthful of honey bun, which Colin hoovered off the floor for her.

"Did you say Delilah?"

Nodding, Lila pointed out the window as a small moving truck drew up outside. Two curvy, young women with long flowing black hair clambered out. Everyone bolted to the window and peered out as the women struggled to open the truck's heavy doors.

Braun stepped away from the window and opened the bakery door.

"Where are you going?" Xandie demanded.

"The truck's doors are stuck, those two little things out there wouldn't be able to budge it."

"So? They're Lila's competition. We don't help other bakers run our own baker's business into the ground." Xandie glared at her too-helpful boyfriend.

"You're right. We should help." Matthew slapped Braun on the back as he joined him in the doorway.

"Et tu, Brutus?" Lila mimed a knife stabbed into her back.

"Won't be long, girls." Braun waved and headed across the road, Matthew at his side.

"That's how that family works. Their modus operandi is flirt and conquer," Elspeth spat the words out, furious.

Winifred raised an eyebrow. "Mother? Do you have something to tell us?"

"I've tangled with their grandmother, the same Delilah the shop is named after. A dark witch who lived to ruin marriages. That was her thing, most of the family are dark or gray witches, but I've never heard of bakers in their line."

"Come on, toots. Give the angst up. The bear and reaper have the hots for the Harrow dames. They wouldn't spoil that." Colin jumped up on a chair and peered out the window, watching both males carry boxes into the bakery. One of the women put a small hand on the reaper's arm and smiled up at him. "Belay that. You girls need to go out and fight for your men. You can't compete with those eyelashes."

Holly chortled, slapping the windowsill in front of her. "See, this is why I remain single. No hassle…" Her words trailed off into silence.

Lila frowned and placed a hand on Holly's shoulder, spinning her around. A glaze of sightless silver met everyone's stare.

The banshee laid her head back and shrieked. An undulating howl of pain. The promise of death hung heavy in the air.

"Geez, that Banshee is as regular as I am when I eat tuna and I bet she can clear the room just as fast."

Colin clambered off his chair and tried to cover his ears with shaking paws.

The mouthy pug wasn't wrong about Holly's banshee shriek emptying a room and the only reason she screamed was imminent death.

Here we go again...

The End.

* * *

Want More?

You can sign up for my mailing list. It's for new releases and no spam. Be the first to grab specials, new releases and freebies.

Sign up now.
https://www.kellyethan.com/newsletter

Did you like this book?

Please leave a review for it on Amazon!
Pies, Potions and Peril

ABOUT THE AUTHOR

I want to thank everyone who spent the time to read my novel.

My world is small town magic, mystery and mayhem, with plenty of snarky laughs along the way.

With an overactive imagination and a love of all things that go bump in the night, it was natural to write cozy paranormal mysteries, but I also love paranormal romance. No matter the genre, I love sarcastic heroines who like to save the day and solve the puzzle.

With a busy and chaotic household, writing is my outlet for madness. I live in Australia and when not writing, I can be found plotting my next fictional murder or chasing after the family's ferocious hellhound.

Visit me today at my website or say hello on social media.

Website:

https://www.kellyethan.com

#8 The Nefarious Nemesis and the Wedding Jinx

Point Muse Cozy Paranormal Mystery Boxed Set: Books 1-3

Point Muse Cozy Paranormal Mystery Boxed Set: Books 4-6

Point Muse Cozy paranormal Mystery Boxed Set: Books 1-8

LILA HARROW: Point Muse Cozy Paranormal Mystery

Cookies, Curses and Christmas Corpses.

#1 Cupcakes, Corpses and Chaos

#2 Pies, Potions and Peril

#3 Sin, Sugar and Shadows

LILA HARROW Point Muse Boxed Set: Books 1-3

HOLLY HARROW: Point Muse Cozy Paranormal Mystery

Banshee, Vikings and Voodoo

#1 Banshee, Death and Disarray

#2 Banshee, Moonshine and Madness

#3 Banshee, Sea Monster and Sabotage

HOLLY HARROW Point Muse Boxed Set: Books 1-3

The Ghost Vein Mine Cozy Paranormal Mysteries

#1 Ghosts and Gold Dust

#2 Curses and Cold Cases

Non Fiction

Heart and Craft.